The inspector silently twiddled his fingers while he thought. Eliza knew that if the allocated funds for food were cut back, the family would have a great deal of trouble this winter.

"Please, sir. We can hardly afford to live as the situation is," Eliza put in, stepping forward.

"Quiet, Eliza," Mama interjected, "this is your father's domain."

"When the ice sets in, we'll have no opportunity to catch fish," Captain Brown stated plainly.

"For this quarter, I'll grant a food allotment for a family of five, as well as pay the salaries of the keeper and assistant keeper," the inspector said. Then he added, with a glance toward Eliza's mother, "That was a mighty good pie."

"Thank you very much indeed, sir," Papa replied, and shook the inspector's hand.

Eliza wondered if it was the apple pie or the inspector's sense of commiseration that had accounted for his decision. Whatever the case, it was safe to breathe once more.

Keeping the Good Light

Katherine Kirkpatrick
AR B.L.: 5.5
Points: 8.0   UG

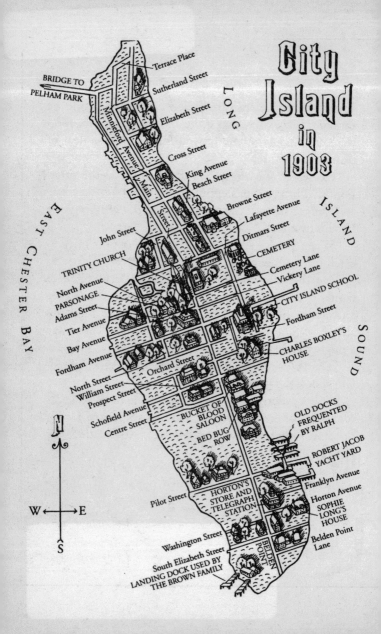

City Island in 1903

BRIDGE TO PELHAM PARK

Terrace Place
Sutherland Street
Elizabeth Street
Cross Street
King Avenue
Beach Street
Browne Street
Lafayette Avenue
Ditmars Street
CEMETERY
Cemetery Lane
Vickery Lane
CITY ISLAND SCHOOL
Fordham Street
CHARLES BOXLEY'S HOUSE

John Street
TRINITY CHURCH
North Avenue
PARSONAGE
Adams Street
Tier Avenue
Bay Avenue
Fordham Avenue
North Street
William Street
Prospect Street
Schofield Avenue
Centre Street
Orchard Street

Minnieford Avenue
Main Street

LONG ISLAND SOUND

EAST CHESTER BAY

"BUCKET OF BLOOD" SALOON
BED BUG ROW

OLD DOCKS FREQUENTED BY RALPH
ROBERT JACOB YACHT YARD
Franklyn Avenue
Horton Avenue
SOPHIE LONG'S HOUSE
Belden Point Lane

Pilot Street
HORTON'S STORE AND TELEGRAPH STATION

Washington Street
South Elizabeth Street
LANDING DOCK USED BY THE BROWN FAMILY

BELDEN POINT

N
W — E
S

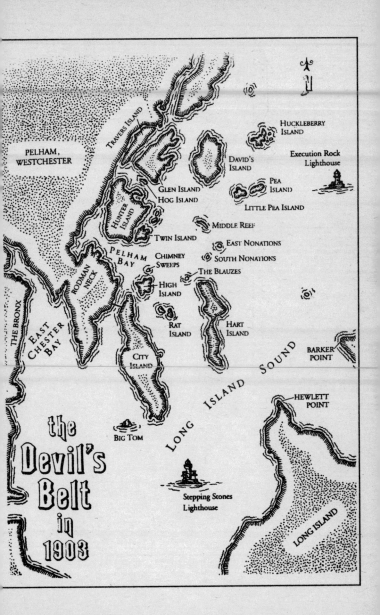

PELHAM,
WESTCHESTER

TRAVERS ISLAND

HUCKLEBERRY
ISLAND

Execution Rock
Lighthouse

DAVID'S
ISLAND

PEA
ISLAND

GLEN ISLAND

HOG ISLAND

LITTLE PEA ISLAND

HUNTER
ISLAND

MIDDLE REEF

TWIN ISLAND

EAST NONATIONS

PELHAM
BAY

CHIMNEY
SWEEPS

SOUTH NONATIONS

THE BLAUZES

RODMAN
NECK

HIGH
ISLAND

THE BRONX

EAST
CHESTER
BAY

RAT
ISLAND

HART
ISLAND

BARKER
POINT

CITY
ISLAND

LONG ISLAND SOUND

HEWLETT
POINT

the
Devil's
Belt
in
1903

BIG TOM

LONG ISLAND

Stepping Stones
Lighthouse

LONG ISLAND

Keeping the Good Light

Katherine Kirkpatrick

LAUREL-LEAF BOOKS

Published by
Bantam Doubleday Dell Books for Young Readers
a division of
Bantam Doubleday Dell Publishing Group, Inc.
1540 Broadway
New York, New York 10036

The trademark Laurel-Leaf Library® is registered in the U.S. Patent and Trademark Office.
The trademark Dell® is registered in the U.S. Patent and Trademark Office.

ISBN: 0-440-22040-8

Reprinted by arrangement with Delacorte Press
RL: 6.2

Printed in the United States of America
March 1997
OPM 10 9 8 7 6 5 4

To the memory of John McCauley

Acknowledgments

Many thanks to my editor, Mary Cash, at Bantam Doubleday Dell, for her belief in this book and for her careful, thoughtful editing, wisdom, and gentle guidance. In addition, I thank my agent, Dorothy Markinko of McIntosh and Otis, for her part in making the book a reality.

I would also especially like to thank my writers' group, whose patience, knowledge, expertise, and friendship saw me through all stages of writing: Stephanie Cowell, Ruth Henderson, Isabelle Holland, Casey Kelly, Judith Lindbergh, and Elsa Rael; and within our larger circle of writers, Jane Gardner, Shellen Lubin-West, and the radiant lady who brought us all together, Madeleine L'Engle.

Grateful appreciation is extended to John McNamara, records historian at the Bronx Historical Society; Norman Brouwer, the South Street Seaport Museum's curator of ships; Ken Black, director of the Shore Village Museum; Dr. Robert Browning, historian at the U.S. Coast Guard; and Hosea Rix, former keeper of the Stepping Stones Lighthouse, for supplying me with background information for the book. I thank Karen Dellinger and Sandra Champion for use of their family painting and for our lighthouse journey; and I thank Chris Baker for providing a photograph of the painting.

A number of other people touched this work in a variety of important ways: Ardyth Behn; Margaret Bock; the Sisters of the Community of the Holy Spirit, especially Sister Mary Christabel and Sister Mary Veronica; Jon Caterson; Mary Cresse; Diane Duryea; Dr. John Allen Gable; Kathy Gibbons; Hunter Hild; Susan Kelly; Audrey

Kirkpatrick; Dale Kirkpatrick; Sidney Kirkpatrick; Jennifer Kirkpatrick-Zicht; Shirley Litwak; Kam Mak; Dorothy Millhofer; Tom Nye; Helen Reel; Jorge Santiago; Catherine Scott; Sanna Stanley; Barbara Stetson; Elizabeth Wein; and Eric Wessman.

Last but not least, I thank Captain Fred "Skip" Lane, whose friendship, encouragement, teaching, and fact-checking were of invaluable aid.

"Keeping a good light"—that is the test by which a lighthouse keeper stands or falls.

—Gustav Kobbé, *Life in a Lighthouse*

The Message in the Bottle

February 17, 1897
To an unknown friend far away—

My name is Eliza Charity Brown and I am ten years old. I live in the Stepping Stones Lighthouse, where the East River and Long Island Sound meet.

It is lonely on this little island. The winters are horrible and cold. On stormy days, rough seas prevent me from traveling the mile to school by rowboat. My chores are to polish the lantern's brass and wipe its lens clean. My sister and brothers and I take turns trimming the wick. The light must never go out lest ships veer too close and wreck on the rocks. Papa says all of us must do our part to save the ships from disaster, and this is what it means to "keep the good light."

Did you know there is a legend surrounding this place? Once the Siwanoy Indians chased the Devil out of Connecticut and down the coast to New York, and he used the rocks here, the stepping-stones, to step, stone by stone, across the water to the opposite shore. On one of the rocks the Devil left the imprint of his toe.

Write if you are able. I hope I make a new friend because on this island I am not able to have friends. Please write soon, as I imagine it may take some time to receive your response.

I enclose a penny for the postage. Any new books and stories you might like to send me are greatly appreci-

ated. I say this in case my letter finds itself in a wealthy hand.

Ever faithfully yours,
Eliza C. Brown

Crouched over the pine table in the lighthouse kitchen, Eliza set down her fountain pen. She read over her letter several times while waiting for the ink to dry. Satisfied, she carefully rolled the scrap of brown paper and slipped it into a blue glass bottle. She corked the bottle, then sealed the cork with the hot drippings of a beeswax candle.

Wrapping herself in a thick red woolen shawl, Eliza scurried up three flights of spiral stairs to the octagonal lantern room of the lighthouse tower. There fierce winds beat against the windows that surrounded a room no larger than a closet. Outside a bell buoy clanked its low, steady warning. Eliza brushed against the great prismatic lens at the center of the room. Using both hands, she yanked open a trapdoor on one side of the room and cautiously stepped outside onto the narrow parapet.

Eliza clutched the iron railing, afraid her foot might slip on the snow of the walkway. She peered down at the immense boulders jutting out of the water, fifty feet below her; then she looked up again. The Devil's Belt, a mass of cold, dark ocean, stretched before her almost as far as the eye could see.

The girl gazed longingly at the thin line of trees that marked the distant shoreline. The tide was high; the bottle would travel fast, she thought. Good. Eliza whispered a hurried prayer: "If it is Your wish, may this bottle bring me a friend." Then she tossed the bottle and watched intently as it hit the water's surface. The bottle seemed lost for a moment, bobbed up and down several times, then disappeared into the swirling currents.

Chapter 1

September 1903, six years later

"Eliza Charity Brown! You aren't spearing eels again with your brothers, are you?"

Mama's stern Irish brogue trailed down from one of the upper windows of Stepping Stones Lighthouse to the giant boulders below. There Eliza and her two brothers, Sam and Peter, speared eels that had been caught in the rocks by the low tide.

"I'll come upstairs in a few minutes!" Eliza called. Well, she'd been found out! Wasn't there any place on this wretched little lighthouse island where she could escape her mother's view?

Now sixteen, Eliza was expected to assume more ladylike pastimes, such as knitting and sewing. Like Amanda Jane-the-Perfect, her sister, who lived on City Island. Amanda Jane had entered into sainthood since she had married the pastor. Fiddlesticks.

"Got him! There's number seven!" Eliza boasted as she drew a long, wriggling eel out of the water. She held it away from herself and examined its spotty, flattened tail and sharp teeth. Then she dropped it into the tin pail beside her.

Eliza marked the wall behind her with chalk. She knew her mother would be furious to see her writing on the wall. As Eliza had often been reminded, all lighthouse property was government-owned. Lighthouse families were subject to a surprise inspection by an official several times a year and could be forced to pay heavy fines for infractions. For this reason, Mama kept scrupulous watch over the household, making sure every surface was dusted or swept, every floor mopped, and every lantern and brass instrument of the lighthouse polished to perfection. But neither Mama nor Papa ever climbed down on this side of their little island.

The tally of eels for the evening was Eliza seven, Peter twelve, and Sam eight.

"Peter's four up on you, Sam," Eliza chided the older of her two brothers. Sam, gritting his teeth, hoisted his spear and pierced the slick, spotted bodies of two more eels.

"Eliza, you're going to be sorry you woke up this morning," Sam threatened. He pulled an eel out of the bucket and flung it at his sister.

The foot-long eel hit the sleeve of Eliza's dress, and black water splattered down her arm. She jumped back. "Look what you've done, Sam!" she yelled. "Wash day's not for another week." Angrily, she grabbed the eel by its slimy tail and threw it back to sea.

"Leave her alone!" Peter warned.

Eliza set down her spear and pursed her lips. Had Sam

6

been drinking tonight? Her impulse was to tackle Sam and kick him, but that would mean giving in to him.

Peter was Eliza's favorite person in the world. Four years older than Eliza, he was kind and even-tempered. He seemed young for his age, though. At twenty, he still had fistfights with Sam. Sam, on the other hand, would probably never grow up. Almost twenty-two, he was a self-centered, reckless, whiskey-drinking fool who collected dead animals' bones for a hobby. He was husky, some thirty pounds heavier than Peter and, at six feet two, a few inches taller. What was more, his anger was frightening. Something about Sam wasn't right. Who would have thought he'd be appointed assistant lighthouse keeper this year, brass-buttoned uniform and all?

Eliza turned to look beyond the lighthouse. In the distance, the lanterns of a ferry glittered like two strings of pearls, and ahead, a few lone lanterns shone from City Island, where Eliza went to school and the family attended church. East of City Island loomed Hart Island, the dark, mysterious tree-filled site of Potter's Field, the burying ground of Civil War soldiers. Above her, the constellation Orion hung diagonally in the sky in all its starry magnificence. Lord in heaven, she thought, I hope my brothers don't fight again tonight.

"Peter, I'm going to drop the whole bucket on your head!" Sam said menacingly.

Sam bent down to pick up the bucket, and in a moment of frenzy Eliza grabbed his shirt and kicked his shins. Sam pushed her away.

"Stop it, Sam. Don't pick up that bucket," Peter said hotly.

"What's the matter, Pete? Don't you want to smell like eels when you see your new lady friend?"

"Lady friend? Do you have a new lady friend?" Eliza asked.

"Maybe I do and maybe I don't," he replied mysteriously.

"Who is it?" Eliza asked, hurt that Peter had not told her this important news himself.

"It's Big May!" Sam barked.

"Who's Big May?" Eliza wondered out loud.

"She's one of the prostitutes from the Bucket of Blood," Sam said, snickering. Out of the many hotels and saloons on the Island, the seedy Paradise Saloon, known as the Bucket of Blood, was Sam's favorite place to have a beer or whiskey.

"Quiet or that bucket is going on *your* head, pal!"

"Go ahead and try it!"

Sam gripped Peter's shoulders and gave him a hard shove.

Just then Mama's stout form appeared in the lighthouse doorway, her hands on her hips. "I think we've had enough of this. Boys, stop your fightin'. There's chores to be done 'fore bedtime," she bellowed. Her presence put a halt to the fight immediately, and Eliza's brothers rose to their feet. "Let's start with the cleanup," Mama went on. "Eliza Charity, have you finished your lessons?"

"Yes, Mama," Eliza replied. Why couldn't Mama stop hovering over her?

"Look!" Peter gasped, and all eyes turned toward the

8

water. An outline emerged of an enormous sloop, its mainmast towering high above the lighthouse. Eliza could tell that the yacht was over a hundred feet long; it was the largest single-masted sailboat she'd ever seen. It was sleek, like one of Peter's boat models. This was no regular cargo schooner. This was a racing vessel!

Eliza climbed up from the sharp rocks and dashed into the lighthouse. "Papa! Come quick!" she called, then ran back outside.

"It's the *Reliance,* en route to Premium Point," Peter said excitedly as he hoisted himself up to the terrace to get a better view. "Tomorrow I'll go see if they need a rigger!"

"Is that the yacht that's going to race in the America's Cup?" Eliza asked.

"Yes, that's her. She's the defender, built and designed by Nat Herreshoff. She's the fastest yacht on the seas," answered Peter.

Presently Papa ambled out of the lighthouse, spyglass in hand. He moved with such confidence, Eliza hardly noticed his limp anymore. By his own admission, Papa was an old, grumbling sea dog, a professional sea captain turned lighthouse keeper. He didn't say much, though he liked to curse, and to his wife's chagrin refused to wash more than once a week. The family passed around the spyglass.

"Damned, confounded vessels," Papa muttered. He stroked his gray, scraggly beard. "I've never in my life seen such a foolhardy waste of hard-earned money as these racing boats. Full-rigged monstrosities, I call them. Unfit for rough seas. Each giant built for one season alone."

9

Despite his grumbling, the glimmer in his eyes showed that Papa was just as enthralled by the Cup races as anyone else. It was the same glimmer that lit up Peter's eyes. Ships. Big ones, little ones, any kind except the modern steamships that clanked and smoked. Sailing excited Eliza too, but she was not hit with quite the same wild fever as her father and brother. Later, she thought, she'd try to draw a picture of the *Reliance* in her sketchbook journal. It was drawing that she loved best.

The huge racing yacht glided swiftly by and disappeared from sight.

"I hate to think of you leaving us again," Eliza told Peter. Peter had been away from the lighthouse often this summer. He was so busy with his rigging jobs that he kept a room at a boardinghouse on City Island. She was proud of Peter for his reputation as the best rigger in the area, but his absence made life at the Stepping Stones all the more dreary. Amanda Jane had married this past May and moved away. For Eliza, having a room to herself and one fewer person commenting on her lack of feminine graces was a decided advantage. But then she'd been left alone to fish with Sam, or to do chores with their mother. Eliza was also responsible for Amanda Jane's chores now, as well as her own.

"If I go away, I'll come back famous," Peter said excitedly. "I might even be made rigging foreman at the yard."

"Sounds like a splendid opportunity for you," Eliza replied. She *was* happy for him, or at least she'd try her best to be.

"Cheer up, turtle," he added. "Ladies' Day is coming up at the Larchmont Yacht Club. I'm rigging some of the regatta yachts, so maybe I could get us a couple of invitations."

"Could you?" Eliza asked. Church gatherings made up her entire social life. Yacht clubs, hotels, and saloons almost never admitted women, and even if they had, Eliza knew her mother would never have permitted her to go. Eliza watched her father turn to follow Sam into the lighthouse, and then another thought seized her. She grabbed her father's arm and said, "Papa? May I row to school tomorrow by myself?"

"Daughter, we've had this discussion before. You realize the currents are strong. The water's cold for this time of year. You know a body wouldn't last long in it."

Her arms crossed, Mama frowned at Eliza.

"I'm sixteen, Papa!" Eliza declared as she stamped her low-heeled boot on the terrace. "You never allow me to go anywhere alone. It's not fair!"

"Eliza knows how to row almost as well as Sam and me," Peter said.

Papa tapped his brass-headed cane. "Tomorrow, Eliza, you shall row. Samuel shall guide you."

Why couldn't Peter accompany her? No, he'd be needed at the shipyard early in the morning and would already be gone by the time the rest of the family started the day. "Thank you, Papa," she said.

"Remember," Papa added, "a sailor has one hand for the boat and one hand for himself. Do you know what that means, Eliza?"

"It means we should always look to our safety."

Papa nodded. "Peter, I expect you to remember this, too, when you're aloft in the rigging."

11

"I won't forget it," Peter answered.

"Come, 'tis time to finish things up here and prepare the Light," Mama said. "Young lady, have you taken the tuck out of the bodice of your school blouse?"

"Yes, Mama," Eliza lied, observing her mother's outfit. Mama always wore a brown dress of the most prudish style, and expected Eliza to dress in a similar fashion.

"Gracious! That blouse has become so tight it's hardly respectable. There's mud on the sleeve of your work dress, I see," Mama pointed out. "I wish you'd leave the eel spearing to your brothers. Another thing: I expect you to act more like a lady and wear your hair up for school tomorrow."

"All right," Eliza replied. Mama was spiteful to tell her to wear her hair up. Her long brown hair and bright green eyes were her best features, offsetting her too-pointy chin and freckled face.

"Look at me. I don't like your attitude, young lady. You're paradin' about with your clothes too tight, and mark my words, you're going to find yourself in a heap of trouble, Eliza Charity Brown!"

Eliza gave no reply and waited impatiently for her mother to shift her attention.

The sun was quickly setting, and it was Eliza's responsibility to take care of the lantern this evening. Papa's charts, speckled with numbers, showed all the shoals and reefs that surrounded the lighthouse. If she didn't hurry to light the lamp, some sailors might soon lose their lives on the Stepping Stones.

Eliza followed her mother into the lighthouse and

climbed up the many spiral stairs to the lantern room. She removed the linen dust cover from the Light's beautiful lens, proud that her father trusted her to care for it. The lens surrounded the lantern like a gigantic beehive, three feet around. It had seven rings of thick glass that could magnify a flame and turn it into a beam that would shine a great distance away. In the last rays of daylight, the glass sparkled and reflected all the colors of the rainbow.

Why wouldn't Papa let her row by herself, she wondered, when he allowed her to do such an important job as keeping the Light? Sam and Peter left the lighthouse whenever they wanted. She was always doing what someone else told her to do. Would she spend the rest of her life doing chores at the lighthouse?

Eliza poured some strong-smelling kerosene oil into the lantern's brass base. Then she opened the door of the lens and used scissors to trim the circular wick so that it would burn evenly. All night long, every four hours, one of the family would climb the stairs to trim the wick and refill the lamp. Eliza now lit the small, teapot-shaped lantern to use for lighting the big lighthouse lamp.

As the sky turned to a deep painter's blue, Eliza joined the flame of the hand-held lantern to the larger lamp's wick. The wick ignited with a burst. Soon the flame became a circle of brilliant light, and the giant glass lens of the lighthouse shone like a burning sun.

Chapter 2

"Sam, you're a lazy sack of bones!" Eliza scoffed. "Aren't you going to help me put the boat in the water?"

"You're in charge today," he retorted. "This is a test to see how well you're able to manage by yourself. Obviously not very well, *Captain*."

Eliza ignored Sam as she took off her gloves to untangle the lines, which she then hooked to the pulleys. It wasn't difficult to lower the dory from the terrace to the rocks below, but it did take muscle. By the time she'd finished lowering the boat and dragging it to the water, she wondered how she'd have the strength to row to shore. Of course, the task would have been easy enough without the weight of her passenger.

Sam settled himself at the stern, and Eliza took her place in the middle of the boat. In another twenty minutes, they'd be on City Island. Land, freedom. With one oar, Eliza pushed the dory away from the rocks out to the open sea.

The morning was still misty and cold, the sky a pale scarlet.

" 'Red skies at night, sailor's delight. Red skies at morning, sailors take warning,' " Sam quoted. Their father was always saying that.

On a day like today, with the water so calm, reflecting the pinks and blues of the sky, it was difficult to imagine the catastrophes she herself had witnessed: a schooner caught in the ice, split in two, and a steamboat and all its passengers completely consumed by fire. Both times she'd actually seen a drowned man.

"Do you think you can hurry it along?" Sam said critically. "If it were me rowing, we'd be there already."

"We'll be there soon enough. Then you can have yourself a drink at the saloon," Eliza retorted hotly. But it was true: She was making slow progress. Her neck and ears were cold because she hadn't bothered with a hat, and despite the flood tide she found the rowing difficult. Sam's weight felt like a rock to her.

"Why are you always so nasty?" Eliza said.

"You're so serious," her brother replied. "Don't you know when people are joking?"

A group of seagulls cried mournfully and circled the boat. Ahead of them City Island came into clear view: trees, a few houses and piers, and sure enough, the *Reliance*. Larger than any vessel in the harbor, it was berthed at the Robert Jacob Yacht Yard, where Peter worked. What good fortune for Peter, she mused. Surely the *Reliance* would need some rigging or repair work before the races.

Eliza looked for the spire of Trinity Methodist Church;

15

in the adjoining parsonage lived her sister, Amanda Jane. A few blocks away from Trinity was Eliza's school. Then just beyond that a bridge joined City Island to Rodman Neck, a mostly uninhabited, thickly wooded land full of deer. A second bridge connected the two islands to the mainland, where roads led northward to the towns of Bartow and Pelham in Westchester and southward to the Bronx and Manhattan. As much as she longed to, Eliza had never traveled on these roads. The view before her eyes was just about the beginning and end of the world as she knew it.

Bringing the dory around the tip of the Island to the landing dock was the trickiest part of the trip. Here, Eliza knew, she must go against the tide while circumventing a reef and a large submerged boulder called Big Tom.

Suddenly one of Eliza's oars missed the water and the dory rocked and spun around. She felt herself losing control. The boat spun around again as she frantically paddled.

"I'll handle this," Sam said.

"No, don't," Eliza said as Sam grabbed the oars from her.

Sam gave Eliza a push and the dory rolled violently back and forth. Eliza fell backward to the bottom of the boat. "Sit still and be quiet," Sam ordered.

You're a big, stupid, useless bully, she thought. A few spiny black cormorants, standing on posts, suddenly took flight. To Eliza, their screeches sounded like jeering.

Five minutes later they arrived at the dock, and several minutes after that Eliza was walking up the Island's busy Main Street, a wide, dusty thoroughfare lined with trees

16

and tall, two- or three-story whitewashed stores and town houses. Each house had its back to the water and looked out to this morning's rush of carriages, bicycles, heavy-laden pushcarts, and groups of uniformed sailors on foot. The City Island streetcar lumbered along, pulled on rails by a black horse and a white horse, Harry and Bob. Eliza waved to the driver, Mr. Pat Burns, affectionately known as Burnsey. Eliza stretched her arms. She undid her hair from its long, tight braid on top of her head, then ran and leapt into the air.

The classroom was already full when Eliza arrived at school. In horror, she realized she had missed opening assembly and that regular classes had already begun.

Eliza could tell by his eyes that Master Crowe was angry. "Come here to receive your composition," he said sternly, his mustache twitching. As she moved toward the front of the room to the teacher's desk, near the potbellied stove, she was conscious of all eyes on her. "Miss Brown, I'd like to know why you bothered to hand in this work to me."

"Isn't it any good?"

"Miss Brown, what possessed you to think these thoughts? How you, one of the school's finest scholars, could have written such blasphemy I just don't know. Please explain why you take up my time with such ideas. Christ being a married man—what insolence! What have you to say?"

Eliza examined the wart at the top of Master Crowe's nostril, which made it look as if his nose were perpetually dripping. She had often sketched pictures of this nose.

The teacher's rigid posture also gave him a peculiar appearance. "If you will pardon me, sir, I said Christ *may* have been married. I did not say he was without a doubt married."

"How exactly did you derive this?" Master Crowe asked.

"Well, there is nothing in the Gospels which says Christ was *not* married. Didn't you say that Christ was a rabbi and that all rabbis and adult people were generally married at the time? Therefore it's remarkable that no one mentions he was not married, if he wasn't."

"Just whom do you think he married?"

"Mary Magdalene."

"Miss Brown, I'll have no more of this," the teacher reproached her. "You're to have a new essay tomorrow. I'd best not find you drawing as I'm lecturing, and I also expect you never again to enter this classroom late. Or else the consequences will be grave. Am I understood?"

"Yes, sir," Eliza said as she turned away from Master Crowe. What consequences? she wondered. She was an excellent pupil, so she imagined he wouldn't expel her. Yet she feared that after graduation in the spring, she wouldn't be asked to stay on as a teacher. Then, with neither a husband nor a job, she'd be confined to lighthouse life forever.

Eliza found her place at one of the back-row desks of the classroom. Her friend Alfred, a thin, wiry, dark-eyed boy, turned to give her a reassuring look. He had a round, pleasant face, wore thick glasses, and had shiny, dark-brown hair that was cut in bangs. Alfred, like Eliza, was studious and tended to be very serious. They often visited

Ford's Candy Store, right next door to the school, for a few minutes at lunch or after classes.

Don't pay any mind to him, Alfred scrawled on his slate.

Eliza nodded and bit her lip. She looked at the faces of her classmates. Most seemed sympathetic, but snippy Carlotta Proudfit gave her a scornful look. Eliza was suddenly reminded of the painful fact that she did not have any close friends among the girls in her class. Whenever she'd had invitations to go to their homes, she'd always refused because she was needed back at the lighthouse. Oh, tarnation to that old Master Crowe, Eliza muttered to herself. As for her composition, weren't her suppositions about Mary Magdalene just as good as the next person's?

At recess time, Eliza raced down the school's stairs. At the foot of the entranceway she bumped right into the most talked-about woman on City Island, the recently appointed first-grade teacher, Sophie Long. Put off-balance, Mrs. Long dropped her stack of books and notebooks on the floor.

"Oh, I'm so sorry!" Eliza apologized.

"Please think nothing of it."

The stylish Mrs. Long gave her a smile as she bent down to help Eliza pick up the books.

Sophie Long was a slim, graceful woman who dressed in ivory and wore her hair in a very long flaxen braid down her back. A bewitching triangular panel of floral lace in Mrs. Long's soft linen blouse curved down to a V at her slender, corseted waist. She was brave to wear a blouse like that, Eliza thought. Eliza wondered what had

19

brought this intriguing woman, a young widow with a six-year-old daughter, to City Island. City Island School seemed such an unlikely place for her. Yet here she was, and she had scooped up the teaching position that Eliza herself might have been offered had the timing been better.

"You're Eliza Brown, aren't you?" asked the pretty teacher.

"Yes," Eliza answered.

"My name is Mrs. Sophie Long and I've been eager to meet you, Eliza. I have heard much about you."

Eliza hastily pulled the shawl over her shoulders to cover as much as she could of her own drab cotton blouse with its purposefully tight bustline. Comparing herself with Sophie Long, Eliza suddenly felt very plain.

"I've arithmetic papers waiting to be marked. Good to meet you," Mrs. Long said, filling in the silence before she gathered her skirts and continued down the corridor.

Well! Let them all talk about me if they wish, Eliza said to herself as she made her way down Main Street to the Robert Jacob Yacht Yard. On the hill overlooking the yard, a crowd of townspeople had gathered to see the *Reliance*. Eliza could see about twenty sailors, all in white uniforms. Some were scrubbing the deck, some were varnishing the trimmings, and others were cutting yards of brand-new rope. She noticed Peter at once, scurrying about the sloop, giving instructions. He must have been put in charge of the rigging.

Eliza had often watched Peter at work, but never before on such a grand vessel. She felt a sense of awe at her brother's talents. Being a rigger meant that Peter was the

20

person responsible for all the ropes, or lines, of a sailing vessel. This required being skillful in working with the lines, but more important, it meant that Peter had to have a vast knowledge of the wind and the sea and how to work in harmony with them.

After examining the lines from below, Peter climbed to the full height of the mast. From up top, he waved to Eliza. By the time he came down again and found Eliza on the hill, it was nearly time for her to return to school. She didn't dare be late again.

"How are you?" Peter asked.

"Terrible!" she said. "Sam was bullying me this morning, then Master Crowe called me to the front of the classroom because of my composition . . ."

"Ah, I never thought much of my schoolmasters. Nor the schoolmasters of me," Peter said good-naturedly. "You know I was always in trouble."

Just at that moment, as if "trouble" had been his cue, Never-Pay-for-a-Drink Ralph appeared through the crowd of bystanders, approaching with his characteristically buoyant step. He made an odd figure in his raggedy black overcoat and his lustrous black hair, which hung out underneath a wide-brimmed western hat.

"Peter, my friend! How do you do?" Ralph said cheerfully.

"Ralph!" Peter answered, and slapped his friend on the back. "I haven't seen you in a year or more. Where have you been?"

"Many places. Alaska, the Gold Coast," Ralph replied grandly.

Ralph, with his clear, dark, shining eyes, slanted forehead, and long, straight nose, was a handsome man. On close examination, Eliza could see that this fine nose was ever so slightly askew from left to right, as if it had once been broken. He had a scar that ran diagonally from one high cheekbone to his full mustache and another shorter scar on his brow, yet these flaws seemed to suit him. His carefree nature was actually what made him attractive, Eliza decided. Ralph was one of life's true enjoyers.

"Ralph, you remember my sister Eliza?" asked Peter.

"Eliza, you've grown to be a beautiful young woman in my absence!" Ralph said, staring directly at Eliza's chest.

"Thank you," Eliza replied cautiously, taking a step backward. Somehow Ralph had managed to move uncomfortably close to her. All the same, she was flattered. It felt good to be recognized as a young woman—especially by someone she guessed to be twenty years old.

"Are you finding work these days, Ralph?" Peter asked.

"Here and there, and I've still to turn in some of my gold nuggets."

"You were mining for gold out west?" Eliza said.

Ralph looked directly into her eyes. "I did quite well for myself in the Klondike gold rush, but then I was attacked by bandits on the return trip. There were five of them against me. Still, I managed to save a few bags of gold."

Peter turned to Eliza and said in a low voice, but fully within the range of Ralph's hearing, "Stay away from drunks and inveterate liars."

Ralph's eyes sparkled innocently. From one of the deep pockets of his coat, he drew a gold nugget and presented it to Eliza with a flamboyant bow.

"I've some business to attend to. A pleasure to have seen you both," he said, tipping his hat and making his exit.

Eliza held the nugget tightly until it became warm in her hand. A nugget of pure gold—here was something, she thought as she watched Ralph jauntily weave his way through the crowd. When he had gone a certain distance, he removed a bottle from his pocket, unscrewed its cap, and took a casual slug from it.

Chapter 3

September 1903, a week later

"You're not still sore about the gala, are you?"

"Yes, I am." Eliza kept her voice low so that Sophie Long would not hear her. How could Peter be so insensitive? Of course she'd still be thinking about not going to the gala at the Larchmont Yacht Club. Women were only allowed into the club once a year. Peter was a bit of a celebrity now as the rigger for the America's Cup defender. After the excitement died down, he'd very likely never be invited to another grand event such as that, either. What was more, Peter had gone to the party with Mrs. Sophie Long, who had turned out to be his surprise new girlfriend!

"Don't be cross. Didn't I say I'd make it up to you? It's rare to be a guest on a racing vessel, especially one as famous as the *Reliance,*" Peter said proudly, adjusting his new white sailor's cap.

Standing at the dock of the Robert Jacob Yacht Yard, Eliza bit her lip as she watched Mrs. Long tie the pink ribbons of her bonnet, which was satin-faced and adorned with an egret feather. She'd never seen a hat with as wide a brim, a great deal wider than was needed to keep a person's face away from the sun. Mrs. Long's blond hair was piled high, except for a single, purposeful curl. She truly *is* beautiful, Eliza thought. It was no wonder Peter was hovering over her. What did she see in Peter? she wondered. Did she actually think Peter had any money? Did she think he was the type of man who'd give her her own carriage?

As the sailors began to assemble, Eliza followed Peter and Mrs. Long down the boardwalk to the vessel. Peter and Mrs. Long made an odd and surprising couple, to be sure: he a gangly and awkward rigger in sailor's clothes, and she a poised, fine lady in a white, eyelet-embroidered shirtwaist and long skirt. She looked like a Gibson girl from the *Ladies' Home Journal*. She was a far call from his previous girlfriend, Anne, a plain and hardworking sail cutter at the Ratsey and Lapthorn firm.

"There are the men from the syndicate, the ones who are footing all the bills. That's Cornelius Vanderbilt and William Rockefeller, and there's Oliver Iselin himself, the manager," Peter said to Mrs. Long in a low voice, referring to a group of men in striped suits and straw hats. Oliver Iselin, a clean-shaven man, was chewing on a wad of tobacco. "We'll let them board the vessel first."

"I've read those names in the newspaper," Mrs. Long said, obviously impressed.

"Who's the woman with the little dog?" Eliza asked, noticing a woman with gloves, a heavy brown veil, and long, full white skirts that reached the deck.

"That's Mrs. Hope Iselin, and the dog's name is

Dandy. She's one of the few sportswomen you'll ever see on a yacht. She serves as timekeeper." Peter instructed Eliza and Mrs. Long to take off their shoes before stepping onto the racing yacht's clean, new pine deck. "I'm afraid I won't be able to stay with you during the sail, Sophie, but Eliza'll keep you company," he said. Then he led them to the stern, where they'd crouch down on the deck with the rest of the guests.

"Aren't there chairs on this boat?" Mrs. Long asked Peter.

"No. In fact, we'll all be lying down on the deck when the vessel is under way," Peter said.

"Why?" Mrs. Long asked.

"You'll see soon enough!" Peter answered.

Eliza snickered. Sophie Long, wherever she was from, obviously didn't know much about boats.

"Is it really true they're going to scrap the *Reliance* after the races?" Eliza asked, showing off her expertise.

"Shhh, Eliza! Keep your voice down. The men from the New York Yacht Club who have paid for the vessel are all around us. That's why we're taking a pleasure sail today, so they can see where their money went."

"But why would they dismantle this fine yacht, Peter?" Sophie Long put in.

"They're wealthy, but not wealthy enough to maintain a vessel like this. Besides, there's no use for it if it's not being raced."

Peter was quick to answer a question if it came from Mrs. Long, Eliza observed.

Mrs. Long gave Peter a playful smile and he beamed back at her. "I'll see you in a little while. Remember to hold fast. That means to hold on tight," he warned her. Then he gave her a peck on the cheek.

Eliza stared out at the blue, choppy water. For a minute, she thought again of the Ladies' Day gala at the fancy Larchmont club. There must have been pleasure boats with striped awnings, dancers and an orchestra, cucumber sandwiches and shrimp toast.

Peter joined the sailors at the bow of the giant sailboat. Just then, the bearded Scotsman Captain Charles Barr took his place behind the *Reliance*'s double wheel. Eliza could tell by the man's presence that he was the master of the vessel. This was the man Peter had often mentioned. He was known as the finest helmsman on either side of the Atlantic, and the *Reliance* never traveled anywhere without him.

Several sailors let go of the lines, then pushed the great sloop away from the dock. Captain Barr's commands were spoken by Oliver Iselin through a megaphone. At first, each of the twenty-six sailors stood at his own station. A few minutes later, when the yacht was pulled out a way, the sailors positioned themselves in two lines and began to raise the tremendous white mainsail, which lay on the deck in heavy folds.

The first mate, elevated above the rest, called out to the two teams of men who stood, single file, on either side of the vessel. "Hand over hand and hand over hand," he bellowed, and the great hoops attaching the sail to the mainmast moved upward and expanded like an accordion. The sail was now three quarters of the way up and billowed in the wind. The men's faces grew red.

27

The sail stopped moving and seemed to be caught. "One, two, three, pull!" the first mate called, then again, "One, two, three, pull!" The men yanked several more times, and then with one final pull they threw all their weight backward and the sail rose all the way to the top of the mast.

With the mainsail raised and the foresail and jib following close behind, the *Reliance* began to fly across the water. Eliza grabbed on to the rail; the vessel heeled dangerously as the sails filled with wind. What a thrill! This was bully! She could feel the speed in her stomach and was wild with joy. This racing yacht was by far the fastest vessel she could ever imagine.

Sophie Long lost her balance and fell backward, and Eliza helped her up. "Mrs. Long, are you all right?" she asked.

"I think so," Mrs. Long answered, her face as pale as her white dress. Her elegant bonnet, still tied to her chin, had fallen to the side of her head and the strong sea breeze was blowing her hair loose.

The sailors were now lying on the deck, lined up side by side in two rows. Crouching down, Eliza watched the low buildings of City Island speedily pass by in the distance. Soon other islands came into view, and then the yacht surged forward into a great open area of the Sound itself.

"All about," Captain Barr commanded, and the *Reliance* turned, its great boom swinging overhead from one side to the other.

"Watch out!" someone yelled as the vessel dramatically heeled and its rail dipped into the water. A large wave crashed and splashed over Eliza and Sophie Long and all the other passengers. Eliza let out a delirious cry.

"All about," Captain Barr said again, and this time, prepared, Sophie Long grabbed on to Eliza's hand as the boom swung over a second time and the vessel heeled in the opposite direction.

"Look how this yacht handles!" Eliza said. Then when Mrs. Long did not reply, Eliza added, "Don't worry, I'm sure we're safe."

For the next hour, the *Reliance* rhythmically rose and fell as it raced through the surf, forming triangles in the Sound. Its enormous mainsail made a thundering sound as it flapped against the wind. People in small pleasure boats waved to the passengers of the huge yacht as it soared by. Eliza enthusiastically saluted them in return.

"Isn't this bully?" Eliza asked excitedly.

"I think I'm going to be ill," Sophie Long said.

In a true romantic gesture, Peter lifted Mrs. Long into his arms and carried her down the gangplank to the dock. "You'll feel better when you've had some food in you," he said, carefully setting her down. "Are you well enough to go to Horton's for some ice cream?"

Sophie Long nodded wearily. She took off her hat and made an attempt to pin up her long tangled hair.

"What a great trip!" Eliza told Peter as she contemplated jumping off the gangplank onto the dock with no one's help. "I had so much fun. I've *never* had so much fun. Peter, are you really taking us all out for ice cream?" she added.

"Yes," Peter said with a wink. "It's your special day."

Just at that moment, all eyes turned to see a raggedy figure with a black felt hat and a long black overcoat strutting down the pier toward the yacht. Eliza realized it was Ralph.

"May I help you down?" Ralph asked Eliza, extending his hand.

"Thank you." She took his hand and stepped safely down to the dock.

"Ralph, you sure have a way of appearing in and out of places when you're least expected," Peter said.

Ralph brushed some leaves off his shirt and gave Peter a mischievous half smile. Eliza giggled.

"I don't believe we've been introduced," Ralph said as he eyed Mrs. Long.

"I'm Mrs. Sophie Long," she said politely, still looking a little woozy.

"I'm Ralph," he said as he took off his hat and shook out his long black hair. Eliza noticed that one of his eyes looked a bit bloodshot. He's such a character, she thought.

"Ralph . . . and your surname?" Sophie Long asked.

"Ralph will do."

As they walked, Ralph's glance wandered across the street and seemed to focus on something Eliza couldn't see. "It's going to rain," he said. "I'll have to sleep in the woods instead of on my boat."

Then, sure enough, Eliza noticed that though the sun was shining the sky had grown slightly darker. "You live on a boat?" she asked.

30

"Sometimes. I've a few places where I go," he answered mysteriously.

"Let's go fishing sometime, shall we, Ralph? We've got to be leaving now, though. Good to see you," Peter said loudly.

Eliza was aware that Ralph was following them as she walked behind Peter and Sophie Long to Horton's Store and Telegraph Station. The favorite gathering place for pilots and ships' officers and crew, as well as the neighborhood crowd, Horton's Store served as a shipping news office, a telegraph and weather station, a general store, and a soda fountain. Its low-pitched roof was topped with a square watchtower, reached only by a near-upright ladder. A watchman sat there, constantly on the lookout for incoming sailing vessels and all foreign ships bound for New York. The building's long open porch was large enough to accommodate twenty or thirty visitors. It was full of men today, a few seated on benches or rockers but most on the stoop, chewing tobacco and exchanging gossip.

"Pete the Rigger!" a few of the men called out in a chorus.

"Deep-Water!" Peter said, and shook the hand of the person nearest to him. It was Joshua Leviness, the lamplighter, known as Deep-Water because he'd go farthest out in the water for his clams. Among the men, Eliza recognized Schooner Mike, Asthma Charlie, Tattoo Charlie, and Limp Ollie. Today, as always, Eliza felt exhilarated to see these men of the sea, who often had a smile for her.

Ralph was greeted with a few hearty calls of "Wild Man Ralph" and "Never-Pay-for-a-Drink Ralph."

The store was one main room that had a wide central aisle with counters and shelves on either side, displaying everything imaginable, from starch, lye, garden seeds, wallpaper, blankets, and dress goods to drugs and salves, perfumes, corn plasters and wart removers, and a Brownie camera selling for a dollar. Near the entrance was a soda fountain with seven stools, where a lean young man wearing a brown vested suit was sipping lemonade and reading the *New York Morning Journal.* The headlines read WOMAN ARRESTED IN NEW YORK CITY FOR SMOKING A CIGARETTE IN PUBLIC and ROOSEVELT OVERSEES BUILDING OF THE PANAMA CANAL.

I'd know those mouse-brown curls anywhere, Eliza thought. It was her admirer from church, the law student Charles Boxley.

Charles Boxley put down the *Journal* and grinned widely at Eliza, giving her a look that indicated there was nothing that could have pleased him more than her having appeared and taken a seat beside him now. Eliza did not know if she was glad to see him or not. His new starched collar seemed a little greasy and he smelled, just a bit, of hair tonic.

Then Charles glanced at his silver pocket watch and excused himself. "I have an appointment with Captain Horton to buy a telephone," he explained. "I'll be one of the first people on the Island to have one."

"Charles Boxley keeps abreast of all the latest inventions," Peter told Sophie Long as Charles disappeared through a back door of the store. "He keeps everything but the Ten Commandments," he said, which was an obvious joke, since everyone knew Charles was an upright citizen and a churchgoer.

With half an eye on Ralph, who was seated one chair away from her, on the other side of Mrs. Long, Eliza glanced at the menu. *Ice cream soda 10 cents. Plain soda 5 cents. Root beer float 5 cents. Sundae 10 cents. Cantaloupe sundae (in season) 15 cents. Coffee (iced or hot) 10 cents. Egg drinks 10 cents* . . . "What a choice, and it's not even my birthday. I'll have a sundae," Eliza said happily to the man with the waxed mustache behind the counter.

"That sounds fine for me as well," a pale Sophie Long, sitting beside Eliza, managed to say before excusing herself to go to the powder room.

"A root beer float," Peter said.

"A glass of water," Ralph chimed in.

"Ralph, since you decided to join us, go ahead and order something. I'll pick up the check," Peter said.

"What makes you think I don't have any money?" Ralph replied. "Water, please," he repeated.

"Maybe there's a free pickle for you around here somewhere, Ralph," Peter kidded.

Sophie Long returned from the powder room looking much refreshed. But when her sundae came, she didn't eat a bite of it.

"Tell me, Mrs. Long. Where did you meet my brother?" Eliza asked pointedly.

"Please call me Sophie when we're not in school. Will you do that?"

Eliza nodded. "Yes, Sophie."

Sophie talked fast and steadily. "I met Peter right here in the store," she said. "My uncle, Captain Stephen D. Horton, Jr., is the owner and I live with his mother, my great-aunt Delia, right around the corner," she said. "It's such a fascinating place with the marine pilots here and all the sailors. . . . Anyhow, Peter bought me a cantaloupe sundae."

So that was the way it got started, Eliza thought. How she wished that she herself had experienced such a romantic adventure in Horton's Store!

"Peter says you have a knowledge of Latin and you've become very well-read on your own. He says you have considerable artistic ability. He also tells me you'd like to teach."

"Yes," Eliza answered, pleased by the compliment. At the same time, she was angry that Peter had told Sophie so much. Exactly how many intimate conversations had they had, anyway?

"Peter said you taught *him* to read."

"Yes," Eliza said, surprised that Peter had divulged this private bit of information. It wasn't common knowledge that Peter often read his letters backward, which she thought was the reason he hadn't performed well in school. "Where were you living before you came to City Island?" Eliza asked, turning the conversation back to Sophie.

"Manhattan."

"Really? Were you a teacher there?"

"For a short time. Yes. After I spent a year in college."

"You went to *college*?" Eliza sat back. She'd met only a handful of people who'd taken the four-hour trip to Manhattan, much less attended college. Sophie must be very intelligent as well as sophisticated and wealthy, Eliza thought. How on earth did Peter end up with such a person? "Don't you have a daughter?" she pursued.

"Jenny. She's nearly seven. My husband died. He was older . . . coronary arrest."

"How long ago?" Eliza asked impulsively, looking up from her ice cream. But as soon as Eliza had said the words she regretted them, as she knew she was overstepping her bounds.

"Three years ago," Sophie answered.

"Don't you miss him?"

"Eliza must be in a mood to ask questions," Peter interjected.

Eliza went back to eating her ice cream, then looked over at Ralph. He was fingering the glass rim of Sophie's ice cream dish. Untouched, the ice cream was now beginning to melt and mix with the chocolate syrup.

"Would you like to have my sundae?" Sophie asked Ralph.

"No, water's fine for me," Ralph answered unconvincingly.

"Please take it, Ralph," Sophie said. "I'm afraid that after being out at sea I don't have much of an appetite. I do wish you'd take this ice cream so that it won't go to waste."

Eliza silently agreed that an expensive order deserved to be eaten. She chuckled to herself as Ralph took Sophie's sundae and made short work of it. When Ralph next looked up at her, his dark mustache was spotted with white globs.

"What are you looking at?" Ralph asked Eliza, using his tongue to lick the last bit of ice cream from his mustache. She noticed that he was missing one of his top upper teeth on the right side of his mouth.

"You're one of a kind, Ralph," she said.

Chapter 4

"Lord above, Eliza. Look at those clouds," Peter said as Eliza took another stroke with the oars on the trip back to the lighthouse. From the stern of the dory, Peter held on to the oars with Eliza to give more power to her rowing. "Maybe we should turn around and stay over on the Island tonight."

Swirling clouds, blacker than soot, pushed through the sky so quickly that they seemed like flames, enveloping the lighter, blue-gray sky around them. "We can get there before the rain," Eliza said firmly.

"It's against my better judgment," Peter said.

"We better just push on, Peter, or Mama will have my hide. I was supposed to be home by six o'clock," she said.

With each minute the sky grew darker, and soon the black clouds loomed directly overhead. "Want me to take over the rowing?" Peter asked.

"I'm fine for now," Eliza said, grateful that Peter was offering to help her and not just taking the oars away.

Then, changing the subject, Peter said, "So what do you think of Sophie?"

"I think you're in love!" Eliza kidded.

"Yes, but don't you like her?" Peter sounded a bit wounded.

Eliza did not reply. She was jealous of Sophie, she had to admit. Sophie seemed so confident of herself, and so free . . . and now Peter wanted to be with her all the time.

"You're going to love her, Eliza. You'll see. Sophie's different from all the girls who have spent their lives at home on City Island. She's not hemmed in by small-town life. She's not shocked by gossip or the kind of misdemeanors that get reported in the newspapers. It's almost as if Sophie has spent years out at sea," he mused wistfully.

"She's hardly been out to sea," Eliza commented. Then she felt ashamed of herself for what she'd just said. The small-mindedness that Peter was talking about was precisely what most bothered her about her own sister and mother, as well as about a lot of the other girls and women she knew. Eliza felt herself soften a bit toward Sophie.

The dory cut cleanly through the water and was at a midway point between the lighthouse and City Island when Eliza felt the first drops of rain on her face and arms. The sky darkened completely. Then it came: pounding rain. In a minute her blouse, shawl, and skirt were wet, and soon she was soaked right down through all her layers: stockings and garters, bloomers, chemise, and petticoat. All of a sudden the wind was raging around the dory and the small boat was rising and falling with the oncoming waves. This was a squall, as sure as she'd ever seen one.

Eliza shrieked, but the beating of the rain was so loud she could hardly hear herself. "What shall we do?" she yelled.

"Squalls usually don't last for more than fifteen minutes. You know that, Eliza," her brother called out.

As the rain continued to beat down, the wind began to gnaw at her frozen fingers and feet, and her wet dress clung to her. The water raged. The boat bore down deeper into the water. "It's sinking. It's filling with water!" Eliza screamed.

"There must be a leak. I don't understand it. This dory has always been very seaworthy."

"Sam dragged it over the rocks this morning."

"You're telling me this now? You didn't check the boat for leaks?" Peter shouted angrily, clutching the oars.

"I looked but I didn't see any leaks," she said. God be with us, she added silently. For a minute the rain abated. Then the squall raged again, the fury began once more. Eliza turned to protect her face from the driving wind and pelting rain. The rain fell so hard she couldn't see more than a few feet in front of her.

"Boat the oars," Peter said. "We'll try to bail her out with our hands."

As Eliza pulled the oars into the dory, a big wave, coming from nowhere, it seemed, struck the boat. A torrent of water fell upon Eliza and one of the oars slipped through her hand. "The oar!" she said. But it was already too late.

"You lost the oar?" Peter said.

Another wave struck the boat, and the lost oar floated to the surface of the water a few feet away. Eliza reached out for it and suddenly fell overboard. The water felt terribly, painfully cold. Then Peter, trying to pull Eliza back, capsized the boat.

Against the current, Eliza struggled to swim to Peter. Peter was, in vain, trying to turn the dory right side up. The rain continued to fall in torrents.

"Peter!" Eliza called out. Eliza could barely swim with her boots and heavy, drenched clothes. She managed to undo her skirt and petticoat and let them sink in the water, but she knew she would never be able to unhook the twelve small buttons on her boots. Finally she grabbed hold of the dory.

"Hold on tight!" Peter called. "Now help me to turn her over."

The dory seemed immovable, no matter how hard they pushed. Shivering and weak, Eliza pushed again and again. Then she lost hold of the boat.

The water was cold, very cold. Eliza couldn't see land and she couldn't see the lighthouse. She didn't know which way to swim. "Peter!" she called out. He must be nearby, she thought, but she couldn't tell. Eliza started to go under. Was she going to die? No, she'd save herself, by jingo. She swallowed some water, coughed, then furiously kicked and flailed to keep herself afloat.

The rain seemed to be letting up, yet the fog was so heavy Eliza could hardly see anything in front of her. She heard Peter call her name. Where was he?

Then she saw him. He had set the boat upright, retrieved the lost oar, and begun paddling toward her. "I'm pulling you in!" he called.

Back in the dory, Eliza bailed out water with her hands while Peter slowly rowed them toward the distant red glow of the lighthouse. What a disastrous end to such a pleasant day, Eliza thought. Out of the mist and blackness, she heard the motor of a launch and saw the approaching light on the bow. There were two shadowy figures in the launch, and one was waving a lantern.

"Ahoy!" someone called. Eliza recognized at once the gruff, beloved voice of her father. Sam and her father had come to rescue them.

Chapter 5

Mama stood in the lighthouse entranceway, a stern figure in brown with her sleeves rolled up and her long grayish auburn braid tightly wound on top of her head. She had been crying. Mama leaned forward, pointing her finger at her daughter. "My goodness, where are your skirt and petticoat? Eliza Charity Brown, I should have never let you go to the Island today!"

"But, Mama," Eliza protested. "Aren't you glad to see Peter and me? We could have been drowned when our boat capsized. Papa and Sam helped rescue us."

"You are a bad girl for worrying your parents half to death!" Mama exclaimed. Then she turned to Peter. "Peter, you shouldn't have been rowing in a squall. I hold you responsible."

Peter said nothing at first. He just leaned forward to give his mother a kiss and hug her. He had a different sort of relationship with his mother than Eliza did, and Eliza was envious of it. "I'm sorry for worrying you half to death," he apologized.

"Stop your snickering, Sam! Take off your sea boots and your wet gear," Mama scolded. "Just look at you all! Come inside, Papa, and shut the door behind you."

"Calm yourself, dear. Everyone is alive and well," Papa said as he gave Eliza a hug.

Mama rushed upstairs, grabbed a mop and towels, and backed down the spiral stairway on her short, heavyset legs. Then she ushered her husband, sons, and daughter upstairs one flight to the living room and kitchen area, where the copper kettle was boiling for a pot of tea. After Eliza had taken off her wet clothes and wrapped herself in a blanket, her mother continued her admonishments while gently patting Eliza's hair dry and removing bits of seaweed with her quick, capable fingers. "You've lost your skirt and I reckon you'll have to wear your work dress to school. Your boots are ruined from the salt water. What am I do to with you?"

Most of the following week, the rains kept Eliza from attending school, though she dared not let her mother find her sitting near the fireplace, reading or making drawings. "The lighthouse inspector should be here any day now," Mama warned fearfully. Lighthouse inspectors frequently dismissed keepers, Mama pointed out, and ever since a local lighthouse keeper across the way on Throgs Neck had been caught serving liquor to sailors, the inspections had become particularly rigorous.

Eliza helped her mother with the scrubbing, polishing,

and whitewashing. In his usual complaining fashion, Sam retouched all the trim on the lighthouse interior with a narrow paintbrush, climbing on a ladder to reach the ceilings while Papa scrubbed the soot marks from the brick chimney. Eliza and her mother lifted all the movable pieces of furniture to wash the floor underneath. They laundered Sam's and Papa's uniforms. Then, for the final measure of preparation, Eliza used the family's last reserve of sugar to bake a crisp pie with tart green apples.

Toward the end of the week, the inspector, an elderly, big-eared gentleman, arrived in his Naphtha launch. Mama charmed him with a radiant smile. She was an attractive woman when she wanted to be, Eliza thought. At Mama's prompting, the inspector ate three pieces of the apple pie, which was kept warm for him in the hot brick oven.

"Have you any additions for the lighthouse library?" Eliza asked hopefully after the man had gone from room to room, running his finger over every surface to check for dust. The book trade was the only good part about inspections, as far as she was concerned.

"This child always was a reader," the inspector commented approvingly. "No new books this quarter, miss, but you can take your pick from these in the sack."

"I'm ready to part with the volumes from the Illustrated Library of Wonders," she answered. "Here, I'm putting back the *Wonder of Optics* and the *Wonder of Ancient Civilizations*."

Eliza fingered through the sack of well-worn leather volumes. She'd already read all of Shakespeare's plays, and there were no novels today, just a cookbook bound with string to keep its pages from falling out and a volume on taxidermy that she hoped Sam wouldn't discover, as it would only encourage him to collect more specimens. Fiddlesticks. Her eyes chanced upon a volume of Hans Christian Andersen's *Fairy Tales,* a favorite book from her childhood, and she selected it at once. Eliza wondered how many other lighthouse children had handled this very same book since she had last seen it. Many light stations were so far from land that the keepers' children rarely visited shore and had to be schooled at home. Wouldn't that be an even more dreary existence than her own?

The elderly gentleman opened his logbook to record his findings while the family looked on uneasily. "No fines imposed," he said. Mama straightened up and smoothed her apron.

"I must ask you a few questions, though, Captain Brown," the inspector continued. "You've told me that your eldest daughter, Amanda Jane, has married and moved to City Island. You have a son Peter, who is not present today. Is he living on the Island, too?"

"He keeps a room at one of the local establishments on the Island, this is true, but if there's a shortage of work he'll be back at the end of the sailing season," Papa said, tapping his foot on the scrubbed and polished floor. Like the floor, Eliza noticed, Papa was especially clean today.

The inspector silently twiddled his fingers while he thought. Eliza knew that if the allocated funds for food were cut back, the family would have a great deal of trouble this winter.

"Please, sir. We can hardly afford to live as the situation is," Eliza put in, stepping forward.

"Quiet, Eliza," Mama interjected, "this is your father's domain."

"When the ice sets in, we'll have no opportunity to catch fish," Captain Brown stated plainly.

"For this quarter, I'll grant a food allotment for a family of five, as well as pay the salaries of the keeper and assistant keeper," the inspector said. Then he added, with a glance toward Eliza's mother, "That was a mighty good pie."

"Thank you very much indeed, sir," Papa replied, and shook the inspector's hand.

Eliza wondered if it was the apple pie or the inspector's sense of commiseration that had accounted for his decision. Whatever the case, it was safe to breathe once more.

With Papa's and Sam's monthly paychecks, amounting to just over eighty dollars together, the family could make the usual monthly trip to the Island to chop wood and purchase supplies at Horton's Store. Mama stayed behind to guard the Light. On this particular Saturday, however, thanks to the squall, Eliza had the unusual pleasure of picking out dress goods for a new shirtwaist and skirt, though all the same she felt a bit guilty spending the family's money. She was even permitted to buy herself a new pair of shoes. With Mama's encouragement, Eliza arranged for Amanda Jane to accompany her on her shopping trip and then come back to the lighthouse for a going-away celebration for Peter.

Amanda Jane and Eliza exchanged hugs on the porch of Horton's Store. Amanda Jane was wearing a new afternoon hat with purple grackle feathers and a satin-faced brim, and new shoes and a new blouse. She wasn't glamorous like Sophie, but she had a pleasant, round face and straight, thick brown hair, and was rosy and dimpled.

Eliza picked out a pair of high-buttoned shoes for a dollar and a half. When Mama was a girl, she'd been told, the shoes did not have a left foot and a right foot. How uncomfortable they must have been! she thought.

"Get the ones with a bit of a heel. Don't you think?" Amanda Jane suggested.

"Mama will be angry."

"You have to learn not to take her to heart. She just worries, that's all. Wouldn't you worry if you had all her responsibilities? It's not difficult to get along with Mama. You just have to learn to say what she wants to hear and not challenge her all the time."

"Well, it may not be difficult for you to get along with Mama, but it's very difficult for me," Eliza said with a pout. Still, she was happy to have shoes with heels.

Together they looked over the dress goods—gingham, madras cloth, serge, taffeta, calico, and damask—while Papa, Sam, and Peter picked out the household supplies and carried them to the launch. Eliza decided she would now wear a blue skirt to school instead of a brown one. Amanda Jane selected two thirty-five-cent bracelets for Eliza and for Mama, and bought herself a corset for forty cents. For the pastor, she bought new woolen hose and new suspenders. Then the two sisters tested perfume on each other and giggled.

"I do love shopping!" Amanda Jane said.

"Yes, I know!" Eliza answered cheerfully. Amanda Jane seemed to have relaxed quite a bit since she had left the lighthouse. Married life, town life, a glorified position as the wife of the Methodist minister, and most of all, having spending money, agreed with her. In a short time, in fact, it seemed as if Amanda Jane's scented toilet water had washed away all traces of her former existence.

Captain Horton himself, Sophie Long's uncle, stood behind the counter when Eliza went up to ask if there was any mail this week for the family. Nearly all the Horton brothers and uncles were highly esteemed Hell's Gate pilots. "Sailors in suits," Papa called those who led ships safely through the rough waters entering New York Harbor. The Hortons owned the entire south end of City Island, including several houses, the store and telegraph station, and a colossal turreted mansion that looked out to Stepping Stones Lighthouse. Still, for all their property, they were a likable lot.

"How's your father?" the captain asked.

"Fine, sir."

"Everything's well at the Light?"

"No wrecks for quite a while," Eliza answered. "And on your end?"

"All's clear waters. I'm afraid there's no mail this week," he said, then quickly followed up, "except a package for Miss Eliza Charity Brown."

Eliza's heart leapt as she unwrapped the brown package. It was a red valentine box full of chocolate-covered cherries! Who could they be from? she wondered. She tried to hide the box, but Amanda Jane quickly came up behind her.

"What have we here?"

48

"Candy!" Eliza said. "I don't know who it's from, though. There isn't a card."

"What is that writing on the wrapping?" Amanda Jane asked excitedly.

The slanted writing was hard to decipher, as if someone had purposely written it left-handed, but Eliza could just make out the words: SWEETS FOR YOU MY SWEET.

"You have an admirer!" Amanda Jane called out. Her voice was just a bit too loud. "Who is it, Charles Boxley?"

"I think so," Eliza said, but then she thought that Charles would not have done something like this anonymously. She really had no idea!

"Well, I'd say you're very lucky if it's Charles. He's one of the wealthiest men in the town!" Amanda Jane said.

"I don't know, Amanda."

"Time will tell. I guess we should head back to the launch now. Oh, I can't wait to see Mama!"

Eliza put the chocolates in the bag along with the dress goods. Back at the dock, her father and brothers were chopping wood. While Amanda Jane, in her new clothes, stood by and watched, Eliza gathered the wood pieces and put those of like size, all facing one direction, into canvas sacks. When they were ready to load up, the tide had started to come in and waves were rocking the skiff. Eliza struggled to keep her footing as the supplies were handed to her—the wood, then the beans and grains, sugar, flour, molasses, canned goods and cheese, and the cloth and shoes she'd bought for herself. Last of all, Peter and Papa brought the big ice block.

"Jeepers, this is heavy!" Peter muttered under his

breath, and grimaced. The combined weight of passengers and supplies threatened to capsize the small boat.

Back at the lighthouse, Peter grumbled again as he staggered out of the boat with the ice block, over the rocks and up the flight of steps.

"Glad that's over and done!" Peter said. He took off his shirt and washed himself with some water from the soapstone sink. Eliza fetched him a towel and a clean shirt, then went to her room to get the picture she had made Peter as a going-away present. Happy to see her older daughter and to have the whole family together, Mama put an unusually generous armload of the freshly chopped wood into the stove.

"Sam, Peter, Eliza, you all sit in the living room for a bit and take a rest. Here's a basket of fresh corn bread, especially for Peter's success," Mama said. Eliza added her box of candy. Mama then escorted them out of the kitchen, giving herself a chance to have some private time with Amanda Jane. Mama had been in a good mood ever since the inspector's visit. Even Papa seemed more gregarious than usual.

Mama and Amanda Jane whispered to each other about Sophie's "peekaboo" shirtwaist with lace windows on puffed sleeves, and her skirts, which were "rakishly high at the ankle." Papa, in rare form, rolled one story after another off his tongue. He talked about his early days as a lighthouse keeper, when a schooner that had sailed from the Caribbean hit a rock and dumped a whole cargo of coconuts into the water. For weeks afterward Mama, then a newlywed, had made coconut pies. Papa had witnessed many shipwrecks in his day.

"Our oceans are a graveyard of ships," Papa said, fingering his gray, scraggly beard. "We must always 'keep the good light.'"

Papa seemed to finish every story with this phrase. The Light was his whole life. As a boy he had been injured in the war but still became a captain later. The navy had found him an early-retirement position, here on the rocky crag of the Stepping Stones. For him, the Lighthouse Service was a true vocation. Eliza admired the nobler aspects of the Lighthouse Service, but she hated being trapped on a pile of rocks out in the ocean. Something else had to be in store for her in her life—but what was it?

Papa excused himself to go check the lantern in the tower and, for the first time in a long while, Eliza felt a wave of compassion for her mother. She tried to imagine Mama as a farm girl from Ireland, slim, pretty, and freckled, with long reddish brown hair. It must have been a hardship for this young girl, who had never learned how to swim, to move to a lonely spot in the middle of the water and raise children there. Even if there had been enough money, things would not have been easy. Then there had been the children who had died. This was something never talked about, the stillborn babies, two since Eliza could remember, but probably one more before she herself had been born. It was no wonder Mama had grown tired and disillusioned. What kind of life would she have preferred? The answer came suddenly to Eliza, and it surprised her. Her mother would have preferred to marry someone like the pastor and live on the Island in a fine house full of china, like Amanda Jane!

Well, enough of these thoughts, Eliza said to herself as

51

she took a piece of warm corn bread and sat in front of the fireplace, near Peter. She proudly handed him the picture of the ship that she had made for him. "Have a wonderful trip," she said joyfully.

Eliza had crafted the ship picture from an old discarded hatbox of Amanda Jane's that she'd found when cleaning for the lighthouse inspection. The picture was a collage made from three varieties of marbled paper. Eliza had cut out a delicate emerald-green two-masted schooner and had pasted it down to sail on a strip of swirling blue water, royal blue with swirling lines of navy and black, against the background of a gold sky.

Peter beamed. "It's a two-masted schooner. Eliza, you're so talented!"

"Look on the other side, Peter," Eliza told him.

Peter turned over the picture. He squinted, then read aloud, " 'To my brother on the eve of the America's Cup races, September 1903. May you always have fair winds and blue waters. Your loving sister, Eliza.' Thanks, Eliza," he said appreciatively. "How did you learn your penmanship so well?"

Eliza grinned. She wondered how, even after all the practice sessions they'd had together, Peter still formed his letters backward.

"I'll say good-bye to you today. Don't look so sad. I'll be back in a few weeks, Eliza, my little melon."

"Melon! Am I so fat?"

"No, silly," he answered. "I don't know why I said that, it just seems to fit. Don't you realize how beautiful you are?"

Eliza shook her head. She didn't think she was beautiful. Peter was the only one who seemed to think so, except for mousy-haired Charles Boxley. Mama said she looked "too determined"—and what was *that* supposed to mean?

"I wish *I* were going off on a ship," Eliza said despairingly. "What kind of life is this for me, cooped up in this dumb old lighthouse?"

"There's nothing like being on a ship, make no mistake, but a ship's no place for my favorite sister!" Peter argued. "You only have a few hours' sleep at a time because you have to get up for watch. For food there's nothing but salty beef. Some of the sailors are an unsavory lot, rougher than the men in the pub. They have tattoos and missing teeth and drink rum from the Devil. No, you're going to have to wait till I'm captain of my own ship someday, and *then* we'll travel in style."

Mama and Amanda Jane reentered the living room and collected the flat basket that had held the corn bread.

"Are you staying for supper, Peter?"

"No, Ma, I have plans," he said, giving Mama his characteristic sheepish grin.

" 'Plans'? Well! You're not staying for dinner on your last day before your trip?"

"Ma, he always has plans these days," Sam said snidely.

"Tell us about your lady friend, Peter," Mama requested.

Peter did not at first volunteer any information, but Amanda Jane, who prided herself on knowing all the latest news from the Island, happily filled in the details, some of which she had started whispering to her mother a few minutes earlier. "As everyone knows, Sophie Long certainly parades herself in the latest fashions from Manhattan. She's new on the Island but she's a relative of the Hortons so naturally the trustees of the school and the elders of the church like her. She's friendly enough and perky, but she holds herself aloof and doesn't go to any of our Ladies' Temperance Society, Church Circle Quilters, or Garden Club meetings."

"If she doesn't go to those meetings, I'd say it's in her favor," Sam added dryly.

In silence, Eliza agreed. If she lived on the Island, she wouldn't attend those ladies' meetings either.

"Sophie was married and she has a little girl," Sam divulged.

"Oh?" Mama said.

"Her husband died," Peter answered in Sophie's defense, "and there's no finer woman on the Island or anywhere."

"Raising a child is a serious matter," Mama said. "Are you willing to take on that responsibility?"

"Gladly, if Sophie will have me," Peter said, turning away from his mother. He glanced at his scruffy and badly tarnished pocket watch. He stood up and took his jacket from a peg on the wall and tucked Eliza's ship picture into his side pocket. "Well, it's time for me to go. Sam, want to give me a ride in?"

Outside on the lighthouse steps, Eliza embraced Peter. He lifted her into the air and set her gently back down again. She noticed how rough his hands had become over the past few years. Of the four children in the family, she and Peter looked most alike; they had Mama's Irish nose and the same reddish brown hair, with just a bit of a curl. His eyes were the clearest blue she had ever seen.

"Peter, I'll miss you," Eliza said.

"You too, sis," he said.

Chapter 6

October 1903

A week passed, then another. By day it still felt like summer; in the evenings the wind picked up and blew across the Sound, spreading the waves into sheets like glass and bringing in, with each gust, more of the oncoming winter. It seemed to Eliza that September had only just begun, and now it had already drawn to a close. The red charter fishing boats at the end of the Island and most of the colorful pleasure boats had already been pulled out of the water. The Island's maple trees were turning glorious shades of yellow and orange. Soon, Eliza knew, the landscape would be desolate and gray and lifeless.

Over the past few weeks, Eliza had received three postcards from Peter at Horton's Store.

Dear Eliza,

Here's the news for the first race. The course was a triangular 15 miles to windward and return. There was a fairly good breeze. The British were hopeful, but we came a good way ahead of Shamrock III, *winning by 7 minutes and 3 seconds.*

> Love from your brother,
> Peter

Dear Eliza,

Everything is going fabulously well. The second race confirmed the verdict of the first. Tommy Lipton put up quite a fight. We came ahead and won by 1 minute and 19 seconds. Keep your fingers crossed for the third and final race.

> Your brother, "the famous,"
> Pete the Rigger

Dear Sister,

We beat the challenger by more than 11 minutes. The fog descended and we lost sight of her altogether. Shamrock III *went a long way off course.* The Cup is ours to keep and last night the hotel orchestra played until dawn. Regards to all and see you very soon.

> Yours, victoriously,
> Peter

"Our boys from the *Reliance* should be home anytime now," Captain Horton said heartily as Eliza picked up the mail. In fact, Peter was due back on the Island that Saturday morning.

"I see you've put out the flags in front of your store and across Main Street. Don't they look dandy!" she said.

"It's not every year we have an America's Cup winner in our midst," he replied. Then he presented Eliza with a thick stack of newspapers and magazines in which the *Reliance* had been featured.

"Gracious! Thank you. My papa is going to love these," she said. The pictures showed the *Reliance*'s entire season: the fitting-out weeks, the trials, the grand mid-summer tour to Newport, and finally the America's Cup races. America's most beloved loser, the British tea merchant Sir Thomas Lipton, was featured as well. He had now lost the America's Cup races for the third time.

"One more thing before you go," the tall captain said. "I think there's a package for you, miss."

Eliza took the package and quickly unwrapped it. Her new anonymous gift was a small, heart-shaped pewter box. BEAUTIFUL THINGS REMIND ME OF YOU, the note read in neat block letters.

"Who left this?" Eliza asked Captain Horton.

"Why, it wouldn't be my place to tell the secrets of my patrons, would it?" the captain said.

The next morning, Eliza attended the service at Trinity Church with Mama. As usual, Sam took them in to shore on the launch, then opted to return to the lighthouse. Eliza and her mother took their places in the front row, where Amanda Jane was already waiting for them. Eliza noticed right away that Amanda Jane had a new, high-collared dress made of pink chiffon, with an ivory brooch at her throat.

"Another new dress!" Eliza said. "You're even wearing a bustle!"

"The dress is lovely and the color offsets your dark hair so nicely," Mama put in.

Mama always favors Amanda Jane, Eliza thought. But then, Amanda Jane did look elegant today—tall and proud.

"Your blouse looks nice," Amanda Jane said.

"Thanks," Eliza mumbled. The new blouse she had sewn had a ruffle at the neck and ruffles on each cuff. Wearing fancy clothes was one good reason to look forward to the Sunday service.

Eliza fidgeted. They were still ten minutes early. The church's one large room was simple, spare, familiar. Eliza liked the round stained-glass window behind the altar, the church's one elaborate feature, but it also made her laugh. Was she the only person who had ever noticed that Christ's sandaled foot in this picture had six toes?

The organist piped a few somber chords while the pastor entered the church from a side door. He was almost completely bald, but his features were pleasant, Eliza mused. He's so old and stiff, she said to herself—too old for Amanda Jane. But if Mama and Amanda Jane think he's wonderful, who am I to think otherwise?

Eliza turned to see who else had come into the church. Several families, along with a few more elderly women, had filed into the room. Her friend Alfred was there, and he smiled at her. A bow tie? He's looking dapper these days, Eliza thought. Toward the middle of the church she spotted Charles Boxley in a brown suit. He was sitting with his mother, a refined white-haired woman Eliza had always admired. Poor Mr. Boxley, she thought. Sweet though he was, he looked exactly like a wax figure. It was no wonder that several young women had already turned him down. Had it been he who had given her the candy and the heart-shaped box?

Then Peter shuffled into the church with Sophie Long, holding Sophie's little girl's hand. They took seats in one of the back pews.

Well, here was Peter back from Sandy Hook, and in church, no less. Peter gave Eliza a self-conscious grin; he seemed very happy. He was wearing the same oversized waistcoat he had worn to Amanda Jane's wedding in May, probably the last time he had attended church. Peter looked awkward when he tried to dress up.

Sophie wore a plum-colored frock. Her blond hair was in a neat coil, tucked into her wide-brimmed black velvet hat. Little Jenny wore a green corduroy dress that was too short for her, but she looked washed and groomed. A fidget of a child, Eliza thought.

"Turn around, miss," Amanda Jane told her sister in a hushed voice as Pastor Lawrence began the invocation.

"It's Peter. He's here!" Eliza whispered.

"Open your hymnbook," Mama said.

The congregation broke into unmelodious song:

> *There is a fountain filled with blood*
> *Drawn from Emmanuel's veins;*
> *And sinners plunged beneath that flood*
> *Lose all their guilty stains—*

"Those are the worst lyrics I've ever heard in my life," Eliza whispered to Amanda Jane, giggling.

"Shush now," Amanda Jane whispered back.

The Prayer of Confession followed the hymn, then a silent prayer, the Words of Assurance, and the Welcome to Visitors. Next the pastor gave the announcements, the Pastoral Prayer and the Lord's Prayer, another hymn, a responsorial reading from the Psalter, then the two scripture readings. I wish I could be sketching in my sketchbook, Eliza thought. Pastor Lawrence chose gambling for his sermon's topic, especially in reference to the local placing of bets on the America's Cup races.

The pastor's an eloquent speaker, Eliza thought, but what a pity he's so off the mark with his audience! She smiled to herself. Does he think the old ladies in this church are placing wagers? If he's looking for the dens of iniquity, he'd do better to go over to the Bucket of Blood Saloon or to one of those raucous clambakes at the Macedonian Hotel. She sighed and crossed her arms.

Pastor Lawrence paused and cleared his throat. "I shall conclude with the Concerns and Joys of the Parish. And I'm pleased to announce the engagement of the widow Mrs. Sophie Horton Long to Mr. Peter Brown."

"Jeepers!" Eliza said. She swung around to take a look at Peter and Sophie. Peter seemed flushed and embarrassed. Every eye in the church was upon him.

"I had no idea!" Amanda Jane whispered to Mama.

"Nor I. You know, she's older than Peter by a few years, and she already has a family," Mama answered. "Still, she seems a decent woman."

The pastor loudly cleared his throat to quell the mumbling before he said the benediction. Eliza waited impatiently for the organ music to start, then leapt from her seat.

Just as she had feared, waxy Charles Boxley followed her out of the church. She darted away from him and found Peter, Sophie, and little Jenny standing under the big oak tree.

"Peter! When did all of this happen?" Eliza blurted out.

"Last night, after I got in from Sandy Hook," Peter said with a grin. "Aren't you going to say congratulations?"

Eliza felt too surprised to know how to respond. Who would have ever thought Peter would actually marry Sophie Long? "Congratulations, Peter and Sophie," she managed to say.

Sophie gave her a shy smile. "Eliza, I want you to meet my Jenny. Jenny may become an artist like you someday. You can draw and paint very well, can't you, Jen?"

The child wrinkled her impish nose and made a face. Eliza was happy that Sophie had called her an artist.

"Someday we'll all take a trip to the lighthouse. Won't you like that, Jenny?" Sophie asked.

"Yes, please visit," Eliza answered.

Jenny's eyes lit up. "Will we ride in a boat, Mama? Can we go today?"

"No, not today," Sophie said, and laughed gently.

"Eliza, would you like to come to Sophie's home with us?" Peter asked. "She's having some family visit from Manhattan."

Eliza wanted to go with them. Just at that moment, however, Mama and a crowd of church people gathered around Peter and Sophie to offer their congratulations. Then Amanda Jane grabbed Eliza's arm, whisking her off to help with the noonday meal at the parsonage.

Chapter 7

"It was *you* all along who gave me those gifts?" Eliza looked at Alfred with disbelief.

"You didn't once guess it?" Alfred said, disappointed.

"Alfred, I didn't know what to think, and I still don't," she answered.

Eliza and Alfred stood on the porch of Ford's Candy Store. Eliza watched the young children come out with their treats: long sheets of colorful candy dots, striped hard candy sticks, licorice laces, hot fireballs hard enough to break a tooth, gooey molasses paddles, and the latest novelty to come out on the market, animal crackers.

"I thought for sure you'd know it was me, Eliza, especially since we always used to come in here after school. Did you at least enjoy the chocolate cherries?" Alfred asked hopefully.

"Yes, Alfred, each and every one of them. Thank you," she said, watching him nervously adjust his round spectacles.

"Why Horton's Store?" Eliza wondered out loud. "Why didn't you leave me the candy at my desk at school?"

"Isn't Horton's where you pick up your mail for your family?"

"Yes," she said.

Nearby Justin, a tall, husky, freckled boy from the lower school, known as one of the bad boys, chewed noisily on a piece of black licorice. Alfred waited for him to go away before continuing.

"So what do you think?" Alfred asked. "Is there any chance of your returning my affection?"

"You're my friend and you always will be. I think we had better remain just friends for now," she said. Alfred was a very fine person, with a generous nature. Eliza admired the way he worked after school every day for his father, the apothecary. If she only fancied Alfred, she thought ruefully, she wouldn't have to disappoint him.

Avoiding his stare, Eliza looked at the schoolhouse. She watched some children file out of the school's front door, which was a rounded archway held up by four columns. This handsome, new three-story red schoolhouse felt calming to Eliza somehow, especially since she hoped she would be a teacher there someday.

"Is it that you favor Charles Boxley?" Alfred asked.

At that moment, a boy ran up the street calling, "It's a wreck! A ship's wrecked on East Nonations Rocks!"

Soon the street was crowded with people, who came from all directions: from Brown's Hotel on the end of the street, the Scandia Inn, the school, the candy store, and

Hawkins shipyard. Eliza and Alfred followed some of the people down past the cemetery to the beach.

"Look!" Eliza told Alfred, catching her breath. About a half mile out in the water was a surprising sight. A two-masted schooner was lying above the water on its starboard side on the reef of East Nonations Rocks. Eliza borrowed the binoculars from a sailor standing next to her and saw two men moving about on the listing vessel. Three more stood on the rocks.

"What yacht is that?" Alfred asked the sailor.

"It's the *Integrity*, en route from New Rochelle to Port Washington, Long Island," the sailor said. He was tall and blond, with a Norwegian accent.

"What happened?" Eliza asked.

"It was a navigational error. You see that bell buoy out there? It looks like the ship didn't go around the buoy, but cut in between it and the reef," the sailor answered. "With the tide already peaked, she's not going to budge. She's stuck right where she is."

Soon the motorized workboat from the Robert Jacob Yard arrived at the scene. Eliza recognized Peter's tall, skinny form among the men on the boat.

"I reckon everyone is safe and sound," Alfred said, expressing relief. "It's rare when there's an accident like this and the sea doesn't claim any lives."

"Yes," she said. Then she took a deep breath, remembering her own recent accident, when the dory had overturned.

Later, Eliza meandered down Main Street on the way to the landing dock. I have to talk to Peter, she thought. As usual, she slowed down as she passed by the dismal boarding-houses known as Bed Bug Row and the infamous Bucket of Blood Saloon on the corner. Since Peter was not among the men sitting on the stoops of the residences, Eliza kept walking to the Robert Jacob Yacht Yard.

The Jacob Yard was an enormous place, several times larger than any of the Island's other boatyards. Where would she find her brother? Eliza wondered. She watched the marine railway system transport a schooner down to the water. This was the railway, she knew, that the financier J. Pierpont Morgan had arranged to have rebuilt in the Jacob Yard as part of a grand real-estate scheme. It was intended that City Island replace New York as the largest shipping port on the East Coast. As part of another such scheme, wealthy businessmen had years before given City Island its name; it had once been known as Minneford Island.

Eliza peered into one of the yard's three huge building sheds, where, in the early evening, the boatbuilders were still working. Finally, she spotted Peter talking and eating clams with Rudy Schofield and some of the other workers. Peter looked grimy and tired, but happy enough.

"That *was* you today, wasn't it, out there approaching the wreck?" Eliza asked.

"Yes. She's a beautiful yacht, that *Integrity,* but I've never seen such a bad navigational error. Apparently the captain was drunk, or else he just wasn't paying attention," Peter said. "Here's some news," he added, becoming more animated. "Robert Jacob has promoted me to the position of rigging foreman and I'll be earning one hundred twenty-five dollars tonight."

"One hundred twenty-five dollars? Really?" Eliza repeated. That was about a fifth of the money her father made in a year.

"Six of us are going out at three A.M. when the tide comes in to tow in the *Integrity*. There'll be me, Rudy here, who's the hauling foreman," he said as Rudy gave Eliza a nod, "Joe the carpenter foreman, and three others. It's a simple job."

"What are you going to use the money for?" Eliza asked.

"I was thinking of taking Sophie to Newport, Rhode Island, next summer," he said. "It will be our honeymoon."

"Does Sophie want to see ships every day on her honeymoon? You're going to Newport so *you* can see the ships there," Eliza teased.

"There are fine houses to see as well." Peter paused and stroked his chin, which was in need of a shave. "So what do you think? Are you going to be friends with Sophie? Or are you going to talk about her, like Amanda Jane and Mama?"

Eliza considered what to say. "I don't know if Sophie and I will ever be friends exactly, but I suppose I've nothing against her," she answered.

"Good," Peter said, and gave his sister a nod. "You and Sophie are going to be close. Inseparable," he added. "You'll see. Just remember, though. You're my favorite sister."

"You always know the right thing to say," Eliza answered.

She wanted to talk to him about the chocolates, and about the rescue, but this was not the right time. "I'd better not get back to the lighthouse late or Mama will be furious."

"Bye, pal," Peter said.

Chapter 8

That night the wind raged. Eliza woke in terror to the sound of ghostly whistling. It was the same high-pitched, constant cry that had haunted her as a child. She imagined that the sound was a chorus of lost souls, singing *"OOOOOOOOOO. OOOOOOOO. Take us H-OOOOO-ME. H-OOOOO-ME."*

Eliza lit the candle of her night lantern, then returned to her bed. "How silly I am," she told herself out loud. "I know the whistle is the nor'easter blowing through the fault in the tower." Still, on such a night she almost believed the stories that her father had told her. She could nearly see the *Flying Dutchman* ghost ship and its crew of skeletons, appearing before a tragedy at sea!

Eliza lit all the tapers in the room and took her sketchbook out of her top bureau drawer. Whenever she was troubled, she turned to her sketchbook. Peter is gone from the lighthouse for sure now, Eliza thought. There'd be no more long evenings spent with him as he taught her how to whittle or paint ship models or name the constellations. But she knew well how to keep her own company. Some years she had even tried, with limited success, to grow a garden on the lighthouse terrace.

She lovingly turned the papers of her book. Between the thick, sturdy papers she had pressed the red and yellow leaves she collected on the Island. She had painted pictures of the Canadian geese as they gathered by the hundreds. One week, flame-colored butterflies had arrived in great swarms, and Eliza had drawn these, too.

Tonight, Eliza drew birds—cormorants, and gulls, and terns with long orange beaks and forked tails. Then, exhausted, but no longer paying attention to the howling and whistling of the night, she fell into a deep, calm sleep.

"Papa," Eliza pleaded the next day. "Tell Sam he has to remove that disgusting dead rat from the base of the terrace."

"Quiet, now. After supper I will talk to him," Papa answered impatiently, turning to Sam.

Sam leaned back in his chair and snickered. "I don't know what she's talking about. I threw the rat into the water a few days ago—"

"Does someone have some more pleasant conversation to offer?" Mama asked.

Eliza chewed a bite of her lobster and frowned. She just couldn't listen to another minute of Sam. Or her parents. Eliza wished Peter were there. What was Peter doing now? she wondered. Very likely he was salvaging the *Integrity* today; the weather would have been too harsh for him to go out last night.

"Eliza, please don't sulk so," Mama said.

Eliza threw her napkin down on the table and stood up. "I'll be back in a few minutes to help with the dishes," she told her mother.

Then, without looking up, Eliza gathered the lobster shells into the tall pot on the table and carried it out of the kitchen. She put on an extra sweater and her parka over that, then shuffled outside to the terrace.

"I have to get off this island," Eliza muttered under her breath. She sat down and dangled her legs over the ledge. The tide was low, the air cold. There was Sam's rat, under the brick base of the lighthouse, hidden from her parents. The rat had already started to decompose and look shriveled. Eliza knew Sam was keeping the rat for his animal skeleton collection. Peter's side of the room had his ship models, Sam's side the loathsome skeletons. Didn't that say everything?

Eliza tossed a handful of lobster claws and legs out onto the rocks. Then she threw one of the lobster heads. First one, then more gulls swooped down. In another few minutes, fifty or sixty gulls were screeching and fighting over the shells.

Such freedom, Eliza thought while watching the birds.

She suddenly heard a motor, then recognized a police boat approaching from the Island. Something must be going on, she thought. Had Sam gotten himself drunk this week and been arrested? Had he hit someone? But Sam didn't have any bruises. Maybe Peter had been drinking! Or had Peter gone off in that storm after all? As the boat came closer, Eliza could see four men, two in blue uniforms and two in white uniforms. Her heart racing, she ran to find her father.

A few minutes later, Papa helped the men dock their boat and invited them into the lighthouse. There was a tall, thin policeman and a fat, bald one. The two other men, wearing white, were introduced as Robert Jacob and another officer from the Robert Jacob Yacht Yard. Eliza and the rest of the family waited in the kitchen as the men talked to Papa in private. The men spoke in low voices and Eliza couldn't quite make out their words, but they were taking a long time. Finally, Papa called the family into the living room. His face looked grave.

"Peter's lost at sea. He is believed to be drowned," Papa said plainly. He paused, swallowed, then continued, "Last night he was out on Jacob's workboat attempting to bring in the wreck of the *Integrity* when the nor'easter came up. Six men went out on the workboat and three, including Peter, were lost."

"God almighty!" Mama cried out. She put her arms around Papa and buried her head in his chest.

"No! It's not true!" Sam argued. "No one knows boats better than Peter."

Eliza stood silently, terrified. She couldn't quite believe what she was hearing. Peter wasn't dead. She repeated the words in her head. Peter couldn't be dead. He was a strong swimmer and an excellent boatman. Surely he was safe.

"Papa, could there have been a mistake?" Eliza asked.

"The whole wreck washed into the sea and sank. Peter was one of the men on the wreck, but we only have the information told to us now, daughter. Hush. We'll talk about it later," he said.

Papa escorted the men to the door and took Mama

73

aside. "I'm going with them now to join one of the search parties. Have Sam take you and Eliza to shore on the launch and you can wait for me at the parsonage," he said.

After Papa and the men left, Eliza and her mother and brother stood together in silence for a few minutes. Suddenly Eliza wanted to run and scream, even to throw herself into the water—anything rather than experience this dreadful silence. She felt too frozen inside to cry. She desperately wished that she had gone with Papa to the Island to search for Peter. Now she had missed her chance. Sam looked about, distraught, and Mama's face was red and she was trembling.

Then Mama squeezed Eliza's hand and said, "Eliza, bring the lobster pot in from outside, please. We'll start with the washing up."

Mama spoke of the plans for the day clearly and concisely, telling Eliza to prepare to spend at least one night on the Island. Mama had said, "Take your Sunday blouse," but she had not said the word *funeral*.

Eliza found the only two pictures she had of Peter: a posed shot taken after Amanda Jane's wedding, and Peter at the helm of a boat. She quickly slid the pictures into her sketchbook, afraid to look at them too closely. Next she packed her pencils, and then her clothes, which she wrapped around her sketchbook. The precious photographs were at the center of the bundle, protected.

The dreadful news had spread fast. There was already a crowd of neighbors and parishioners waiting at the parsonage when Eliza and Mama arrived. Amanda Jane rushed out to greet them. Pastor Lawrence kissed Mama and Eliza.

"I'm going to try to find Peter," Eliza said, setting down her bag.

"There are several search parties already out, dear," the pastor said kindly. "Please come inside."

"No. I've got to find him!" she said frantically. Then Eliza ran across the Island as fast as her legs could carry her, with Amanda Jane and Mama calling her name. In a few minutes she was on the beach, from which she had first seen the wreck just a day earlier.

All she could see was calm blue water, without a single breaking wave or boat. The only sign of the wreck was the debris that crowded the beach: logs, timber, planks, seaweed, nails, pieces of wet fabric, bottles, a soggy shoe. Eliza picked up the shoe, but it wasn't Peter's. She stood next to the water. As she turned toward town, two bearded, scruffy-looking men in a lobster boat came up to the beach. Eliza ran toward them.

"What's the matter?" one of the men asked.

"I have to find the *Integrity*," Eliza answered.

"About half an hour ago," the lobsterman told her, "a big derrick barge removed the wreck. She's on the way to the Robert Jacob Yacht Yard."

Eliza thanked the lobstermen and ran all the way, a half mile down Main Street, to the yard. There, in the boatyard's basin, a huge crane barge was lifting the wreck of the *Integrity* onto the land. Eliza pushed through the crowd of bystanders. The wreck, hanging by two large

75

slings, was hoisted above the waterline. Water gushed out of the huge holes where the pinnacles of the rocks had punctured the hull.

"Stand back! Everyone stand back!" one of the workers from the shipyard called out.

Chapter 9

Papa appeared in the crowd and saw Eliza. "What are you doing here?" he asked. "I thought you were at the parsonage."

"I couldn't stay away."

Papa nodded, his face looking tired and grave. He took Eliza's hand and seemed about to speak when a group of men carried two large corpse-shaped burlap bags from the derrick. They loaded the bodies onto a long black wagon, pulled by four horses, that said FORDHAM MORGUE.

"Oh, Papa!" Eliza said, and screamed. She tried to run toward the wagon, but he held her back.

"They found Peter when they raised the wreck. He was trapped in the after-cabin. One of the other men, Rudy Schofield, was found lashed to the mast. I'm sorry, daughter . . ."

"Peter!" Eliza shrieked. "No! No!"

Papa held her as she beat her fists against his thick chest. Then he embraced her tightly while she cried, and

Eliza could tell he was holding back his own tears. "There never was a man so dear as our Pete," he said.

The crowd moved aside to make way for the morgue wagon, and Eliza pulled away from her father to get a closer look. The wagon had no windows, so it was impossible for Eliza to get a view of Peter before the wagon rolled up the hill to Main Street. A chill passed through her body as she listened to the dull clumping sounds of the horses' hooves.

"Where are they taking him, Papa?" Eliza asked.

"He's going to Fordham for an autopsy. I'll have to identify him there today. Then, probably tomorrow, I'll have him brought back to the Island," Papa answered slowly.

Eliza studied the deep, pained wrinkles across her father's brow. "Why Peter, Papa? He's the last person in the world I'd want to die. I'd rather have died myself."

"We're going to be all right, daughter," Papa said. "God only knows how, but we're going to survive this."

That night Eliza lay awake in her room at the parsonage. She couldn't cry. She prayed a few times. Then she got out of bed, lit the lantern, and wrote the date in her sketchbook journal. *Saturday, October 24, today, Peter was found dead.* She took a blank page and inked in a big cross. Eliza shuddered as she remembered the shrill wailing that had awakened her the night before: The *Flying Dutchman* ghost ship had given its warning.

Toward dawn Eliza drifted into a light sleep that lasted only a short time. She woke disoriented and did not at first remember what had happened. But the dull ache in her stomach reminded her that something was terribly wrong. Then she remembered: Peter's dead.

She got herself out of bed and looked out the window. Outside, a thin mist was rising from the green fields in back of the parsonage. It was raining lightly. "God grant me the strength to live through the day," she whispered.

By afternoon, a crowd had gathered at the parsonage to pay their respects to the family. It was a comfort to feel the loving arms of the community, yet there was a hollowness inside Eliza that nothing could fill. How strange and disconcerting, she thought, for the quiet, staid house of the pastor—a home with marble fireplaces and porcelain doorknobs—to be so full of noise and confusion. There were people of all types in the parlor today; the older women of the church were seated alongside sailors and shipyard workers, who were smoking pipes, reaching into snuffboxes, and talking in Scandinavian languages. Amanda Jane looked pale and sickly to Eliza during this time, and Mama appeared to exist on sheer nerves, rushing about and hurriedly greeting visitors.

Alfred stopped by briefly. So did waxy Charles Boxley. Eliza could not muster up enthusiasm for small talk. Even Ralph made an appearance, his muddy boots leaving large tracks on the pastor's Persian rug. He was seated hunched over with his long hair hanging down, unabashedly weeping. It moved Eliza to see Ralph this way—he must have deeply loved his boyhood friend. Peter had been a favorite to all, this was clear. Eliza avoided Ralph, helping Amanda Jane and Mama in the kitchen, making tea, and serving the food the neighbors brought. When she looked for Ralph again, he was gone.

Soon after Ralph's departure Sophie arrived at the parsonage. Just the sight of her made Eliza melt inside. She looked at Sophie as if it were for the first time. Sophie, so pretty, her face red from crying, had her arms outstretched just for her, Eliza. Sophie's heart is like a field of goldenrod and Queen Anne's lace, Eliza thought. I've not been fair to her. In Sophie's arms, Eliza suddenly let go and broke into a fit of tears. "No, this isn't happening," she sobbed.

Late that day Papa returned looking haggard. He'd arranged for Peter's body to be cared for at Pine and Rice Undertakers on Main Street. Eliza wished she could see Peter again, see his face, to make sure that two days ago she had really had a beloved brother. She sat on the parsonage sofa with Papa and pored over the charts of the local waters around East Nonations Rocks. She needed to know the details of the tragedy.

"What happened, Papa?" she asked. She knew that her father had talked to one of the three survivors of the wreck.

Papa placed his finger on the chart. Mama stood over them, watching. "The workboat was here and the *Integrity* was here," he said, moving his finger. "Two of the six men stayed on the workboat to handle the lines. The four others, including Peter, boarded the wreck to secure the lines. The workboat was probably just about to pull the wreck off the rocks when the storm came up so suddenly."

"But why did the wreck sink?" Eliza asked.

Papa anxiously rubbed his scraggly gray beard. "The tide was already flooding. Then the storm made the waves even higher. The waves pushed the hull of the boat against the rocks, again and again. Water poured in through the holes the rocks made and the boat went down. All at once."

"Do you think Peter died quickly?"

"Yes," said Papa. He sighed deeply. Mama stood over him and put her hands on his shoulders. She was trembling, and her face had turned white.

Every question led to another question, but none of the facts made Peter's death seem real to Eliza. All the same, hearing the details was giving her a pain in her guts.

"When the storm came up, the hauling foreman, Rudy Schofield, was struck by a giant wave," Papa continued. "Mr. Schofield was slammed against the mast and was left unconscious. Peter tied him to the mast to try to save him. Then Peter must have run below for cover. Both of them drowned when the boat went down."

So Peter had died trying to save his friend Rudy. "What about the other two men who were on the wreck?" Eliza asked, her voice breaking.

"They were washed overboard. One is still missing. The other man, who was wearing a life preserver, miraculously swam ashore over a mile away on Sands Point, Long Island. He lived."

"It's time we leave," Mama told Papa.

Eliza wanted to hear more. "No, Papa, wait. What was Peter wearing when they found him?"

"You don't need to know these things, Eliza," Mama said.

Papa did not answer at first; then he told her. "Rubber boots, gloves, a pea jacket, his heavy gray sweater, trousers, socks, an oilskin suit outside of everything, and a pilot cap pulled down over his ears."

So he had worn a hat. Eliza was somehow comforted to hear he had been warm before he hit the water—although what did it matter now? Papa showed her Peter's wallet, and in it were four damp dollar bills. Papa would say no more, but later, Eliza overheard him tell one of the men that Peter's skin had turned an icy blue.

Exhausted, Mama accompanied Papa home to the lighthouse. Mama thought it better that Eliza stay at the parsonage to help Amanda Jane, who was not feeling well and was now in her room.

The next day passed slowly, but in the evening more neighbors arrived at the parsonage. The man lost in the Sound had been found dead.

That night Sam staggered into the parsonage. His hair looked greasy and his clothes disheveled. He smelled of sweat and tobacco, and at the sight of him everyone in the parlor became absolutely still. The pastor looked up from the desk where he was writing. Little Jenny, on the Persian rug, stopped playing with her doll.

Sam paced back and forth in front of the pastor's marble fireplace, his face red and his eyes wild.

"Sam, please sit down," the pastor said sternly.

Sam continued to pace. "He's not dead. I just know he's not dead."

"Come, sit near me, Jenny," Sophie said, drawing her daughter to her.

Eliza stood up and walked over to Sam, then studied him for a moment in silence. His jawline was similar to Peter's, though his face was square.

82

Sam gave Eliza a look as if to say, Stop staring at me!

Eliza continued to stare. Then she smiled at him, saying in her mind, I love you, Sam. Though I hate you, I love you. You are my own dear brother, my own blood.

"Turn around," Sam said, slurring the words. For the first time, Eliza noticed fear in his eyes. The realization came upon her quite suddenly: Sam was afraid of her! Sam had been afraid of her all along.

"Sam, go lie down. You're drunk," she said.

He grabbed her by the wrists and squeezed them so hard that she cried out in pain.

"I'm not drunk! What is everyone so upset about? Everyone stop staring at me!" he shouted.

"Let me go," Eliza said calmly, "please."

Pastor Lawrence rose from his chair. "Let her go, Sam."

"Don't tell me what to do," Sam warned. He released Eliza and stepped toward the pastor. "One more word from you and I'm going to smack you across the face!"

"Mama, I want to go home," Jenny said.

"Yes. Put on your coat, miss," Sophie told Jenny.

Sam started to pace again and, tripping on Jenny's little doll, fell to the floor.

"Get this runty little child away from me!"

Jenny shrieked and ran to her mother.

Eliza drew a deep breath. "God help you, Sam," she said, feeling her heart race. She knew there was no reasoning with Sam when he had the drink in him. No reasoning at all.

Sam was on his feet again and standing near the doorway. He had a peculiar look on his face and was gazing into the air in front of him.

"It's Peter. He's here," Sam said more quietly. "He says he's sorry for the arguments we had. He says it's all right now, we can part as friends. He seems so happy."

Eliza looked to the place where Sam's eyes were fixed, but did not see anything but the fireplace and above it a picture of a cathedral surrounded by grazing sheep.

"He's leaving now," Sam said. "Don't you see him? Can't you feel the heat? He's going across the room at a diagonal. He's right in front of the fireplace. Now he's gone."

Without warning, Sam turned around sharply and, with his full force, punched his fist into the door.

"Damn! Damn!" he cried out. His knuckles bled.

Pastor Lawrence helped Sam to the couch, and Sophie took the opportunity to slip out the door with her daughter. Sam sat by himself, his head on his knees, and cried with great intensity. The danger had passed now; Eliza felt it. Sam would not give them any more trouble tonight. In a few minutes he would fall asleep, just as soon as his weeping exhausted him.

After the funeral, visitors stopped coming by. Five miserable days at the parsonage passed. Eliza woke still feeling tired and empty on the sixth morning, but a bit stronger as well. She realized she soon would have to return to school and to her life.

"You've lost weight and the life's gone out of you. You're pale, just like your sister. Why don't you go outdoors?" the pastor suggested over breakfast.

The pastor gave Eliza permission to ride Amanda Jane's bicycle. This fancy lady's-style bicycle, with its two large wheels at the back and one small wheel in the front, had been the pastor's wedding gift to his wife. But Amanda Jane disliked all sports and had been hoping instead for a sewing machine. She had never ridden the bicycle. Now, with just a little practice, Eliza felt confident enough to take it out on her own.

The day was unusually warm for early November. Eliza pedaled down Main Street and waved to the children playing stickball. A tear rolled down one cheek as she thought of Peter. She would never, ever see his sparkling blue eyes again. How was it, she wondered, that although she felt sick and miserable, her senses had become so keen?

"Peter, I see the world today and feel a part of it," she said. "There's joy in pain and pain in joy, isn't there? I never realized it before, and yet it is the truth." Then, as Eliza crossed City Island Bridge, she felt a burning in her heart and the water looked a deeper blue than it had ever looked to her before.

Chapter 10

November 1903

"I'm pregnant," Amanda Jane announced the next day. Totally surprised, Eliza nearly dropped the orange chrysanthemums she was holding. "Mama is going back to the lighthouse this afternoon," Amanda Jane continued as the two sisters headed down Main Street toward the cemetery. "We've arranged that you are to live with me and help out at the parsonage."

"What does this mean?" Eliza asked. Her throat felt suddenly hoarse and her eyes tired and heavy.

"Our home will be your home."

"I'm going to live with you? That's good news . . . I suppose. I don't know what to say. . . . A baby! How wonderful!" Eliza swallowed. "When will you give birth?"

"In late April or early May."

Eliza froze in her tracks, taking in the news, which she was certain she'd need some time to sort out. Good Lord, living on the Island was what she had always wanted. She felt for a second a burst of hope. But she wondered what it was going to be like living in the same house with a stodgy clergyman. She noticed that her sister was walking more slowly than usual, struggling up the hill of Fordham Avenue to the little cemetery that overlooked the Sound and Hart Island. Though she hadn't realized it before, she could now tell quite clearly that Amanda Jane was indeed pregnant.

They approached Peter's grave, a simple wooden cross near a series of small tombstones that marked the places of the infants in the family who had died. Eliza bent down and lovingly laid the chrysanthemums on the grave as she felt the first raindrops fall on her back.

Then it suddenly occurred to Eliza that no one had consulted her about this terribly big decision, and she became upset. "I don't understand, Amanda," she said, feeling a headache coming on. "Tell me, when was it discussed that I live with you?"

"Yesterday, when you were off on that bicycle. Then Mama and I talked again last night."

"Why didn't anyone ask me first?" Eliza inquired.

Amanda Jane sighed and turned away for a moment. She looked hurt. "Wouldn't you rather live with me?"

"Yes, of course. You know I would, but . . . you might have asked."

"It's settled, then. There's one more thing! Miss Higgins, the school's fourth-grade teacher, has taken ill. Sophie suggested to the principal that you teach the class for a few weeks. You would make up your own schoolwork independently, and you'd even receive a small stipend."

"Me? They want me to be the teacher?" Eliza asked, shocked. She could hardly believe the news! It was a dream come true, and yet she couldn't quite feel happy

87

about anything, now that Peter was gone. She'd always imagined he'd be there with her to share in any good things that might happen.

"Maybe this isn't the right time—"

"Nonsense. You'll be a wonderful teacher," Amanda Jane reassured her. "Doesn't Papa always say 'Don't wait until you're ready'? Mama and I have talked it over and we feel it will be good for you to have some more responsibility of your own. Now, before it rains any harder, we must go to Peter's room and collect his things."

"The idea of going there is almost more than I can bear," Eliza said sadly. At the same time, she felt compelled to go. Being in Peter's room, she hoped, might help her remember what it had been like to be with him.

"It's painful, I know, but we'll make a quick trip and it will soon be over. At least we'll be together," Amanda Jane said, and squeezed Eliza's hand as they headed back.

In a few minutes they were back on Main Street, and, catching sight of Burnsey and his horse-drawn trolley, they decided to take the slow, bumpy ride down the street rather than walk in the rain. Eliza pushed her way into the packed car, and as all the seats were taken, they stood. Eliza held her breath to keep from having to smell the stench of whiskey breath and tobacco juice. The trolley soon came to a screeching halt across from the boarding-house, and Eliza felt an enormous sense of dread as she stepped down onto the street.

Amanda Jane took Eliza's arm protectively as they reached the Bucket of Blood Saloon. Eliza strained to peer into the saloon's dark windows, but the oval panes of red stained glass, etched with fancy scrolls, kept her from seeing through to the other side. Amanda Jane warned her, "We can't be seen near this place."

"Why are you worried? What's the difference if we're seen?" Eliza asked. Amanda Jane pulled her along, quickening their pace. The rain was falling quite steadily now.

"One has one's place in society, and that means, my dear, that the wife of the pastor, and the sister-in-law of the pastor, should not be seen near saloons and houses of ill repute. Eliza, perhaps it was my mistake that we venture out this afternoon without a chaperone. Perhaps it would have been better to wait. Yet I feel in my heart we should pick up Peter's things right away. The sooner we proceed with our lives the better."

Around the side of the Bucket of Blood was the entrance that led to the upstairs rooms of the boarding-house, which had no name but was known throughout town as Bed Bug Row. Eliza listened to the raucous voices and piano music coming from the saloon as they climbed the two flights of stairs. The hallways were dingy and in need of paint and repair. It was awful to be in this place with Peter gone, she thought. She couldn't think of anything more terrible, then remembered seeing the two bodies carried off the wreck. She hesitated for a moment before pushing open the narrow door to Peter's room.

For a minute Eliza half-imagined she might see Peter's ghost. At least a ghost would be something, she said to herself. It would be better than the nothingness that she carried around with her.

The room was just a high-ceilinged attic, furnished very sparsely with a bed, chair, lamp, and chipped porcelain sink. The attic had six windows, several cocked open at the top. Light jets of rain, blown by the wind, fell upon Peter's bare mattress and worn, soiled blankets. Some of the work clothes that Eliza remembered Peter having worn the previous week lay in a pile on the floor. The bleak scene filled Eliza with sadness, and Amanda Jane, too, seemed shaken.

"Just think," Amanda Jane said, and sighed. "If Peter had lived another week, he'd have moved to Brown's Hotel, a good, reputable place. He had so much to look forward to! He had a new position at the shipyard and he was engaged. I had no idea he was living in such squalor here."

"I didn't know either," Eliza said, though she had guessed it. If he had not given his money to the family, he certainly could have lived in any of a dozen hotels on the Island. She wondered how often he'd caroused with the sailors in the saloon downstairs.

"It will be a simple task to collect his belongings. I imagine we can fit his possessions into one sail bag," Amanda Jane said, and wiped a tear with her embroidered handkerchief.

Eliza took down the row of pictures that hung diagonally along the slanted eaves and found a small photograph of the family at Amanda Jane's wedding, as well as the picture of the schooner she had made for Peter's going-away party. Next Eliza noticed a photograph of Sophie in one of her fancy plumed hats. Eliza carefully collected the little pieces of the model sailboat Peter had been constructing and gazed out the window to Hansen's Yacht Yard, where men were hauling boats out of the water. Eliza wished that she, like the boats, could remain sleeping through the long winter, a hollow hull turned over and covered by canvas.

Suddenly dizzy, Eliza sat down on Peter's damp, musty mattress and held her head with both hands. She was cold and wet; her feet were numb. Some time passed before she had the vague sense that someone was talking to her.

"Come now, it's time we go home," Amanda Jane said gently.

"Being here was too much for me. I feel ill."

"I know. It's awful, isn't it? Like a wave that hits you and knocks you over," Amanda Jane said, sitting down beside Eliza and putting her arm awkwardly around her. In that moment Eliza felt close to her sister, as she sometimes did. Today Amanda Jane hadn't criticized her once and had acted with unusual tenderness.

"Peter has been dead less than a week. Now I'm not going home. I'm to be a teacher. My whole life has changed, Amanda Jane!"

"Mine, also. The changes have all come too fast."

"I'm happy about the baby."

"Yes, I am, too. Lawrence says that when God takes something away from us, He always gives us something in return."

Eliza turned those words over in her head. They seemed to her words in another language. Something in return, she thought. How could anything ever replace what was lost? Just then she would have given anything in the world to have Peter back again.

Chapter 11

"I want to know why you suggested *me* as the teacher," Eliza said to Sophie. Sophie had come to the parsonage that evening to help Eliza study the fourth-grade lessons in the McGuffey reader and outline her first week's work of reading, grammar, penmanship, history, geography, and arithmetic. Now most of the work was completed, and Eliza began to fit the nibs into her pupils' wooden pens. For a little while, the pastor had stayed on in the adjoining parlor reading his newspapers by fishtail gaslight, and perhaps eavesdropping. Then he said his good nights and joined his wife in their bedroom down the hallway.

"I recommended you because you're a young woman of great enthusiasm and vitality. You're perfect for the position!" Sophie declared, and scribbled a few more thoughts in Eliza's notebook. "Peter had told me how you taught him to read when no one else could."

"Well, I hope I don't disappoint you," Eliza commented. She laid down a pen on the lustrous mahogany dining room table. "I bet it took considerable convincing on your part before the principal wanted me," Eliza said, probing a bit further.

"No, not exactly. You're known as a very fine scholar."

"Still, I hardly expected—"

"Don't you think *I'm* a little out of the ordinary for a schoolteacher?"

"Yes, you are," Eliza answered without hesitation. All you had to do was look at her sitting there to see that Sophie was a rare bird, Eliza thought. Besides, it wasn't exactly regular for a stranger from off the Island to be invited to teach at the City Island School. If you weren't from the Island then you weren't a "clam digger," and that made you suspect.

Sophie rolled up her frilly sleeves and looked straight at Eliza. "Don't fret about all the details we've gone over tonight," she said. "Just remember this: The most important thing about teaching is that you show joy and enthusiasm. If you truly enjoy what you present, your pupils will enjoy it, too. Fourth grade is a wonderful grade. I taught it once."

Eliza stacked up the twenty-one pens, then got up to throw another log on the fireplace. "What activities did you do with your fourth-grade class?" Eliza asked.

"All sorts of things. We made cuneiform clay tablets and medieval felt banners. We built the Seven Hills of Rome out of papier-mâché, and wrote letters to imaginary Roman friends and relatives. Sometimes we told stories and enacted them as plays."

"You did those things?" Eliza asked, surprised at how imaginative Sophie was, not only in her style of dress but, it appeared, in her style of teaching as well.

"Certainly. I wish you could watch me teach for the next few days. You'd see that my classes also have their fair share of memorizing passages and doing arithmetic; I do have my rules, of course. Which reminds me," Sophie said, then fumbled for something in her purse. "I'm supposed to give you a copy of the *Rules for Teachers*."

"Rules for teachers?" Eliza repeated. "I didn't know there were any. Now I've *true* reason to be nervous."

"Nonsense! They're only the principal's guidelines, which you abide by already. You have nothing to worry about," Sophie said as she handed Eliza a yellowing two-page typewritten document.

Eliza quickly glanced over the pages, then began to read them more carefully. Some of the rules were to fill the lamps with kerosene and clean the chimney, to bring a bucket of water and a scuttle of coal each day, and things like that. Other rules involved social mores. " 'Four. Men teachers are permitted one evening each week for courting purposes, or two evenings a week if they go to church regularly,' " Eliza read out loud. "I didn't know that was a rule!"

"That rule isn't for women. Keep reading," Sophie said.

" 'Five. After the school day, the teachers are requested to spend the remaining time reading the Bible or other good books. Six. Women teachers who engage in improper conduct will be dismissed. Seven. Any teacher who smokes; drinks liquor; visits clubs, pool halls, or public halls; or gets shaved in a barbershop will give good reasons for people to suspect his worth, intentions, and honesty.' Jeepers! It sounds as if I'm going to be watched!"

"Don't fret, Eliza," Sophie repeated earnestly. She reached out and brushed back some hair that was hanging in Eliza's face. "The principal is a good and gentle man, and he told me himself that he thinks highly of you."

Eliza formed a picture in her mind of the small, elfin principal, Hosiah Prim, who had a nearly bald head, a goatee, and twinkling blue eyes. No, he wasn't threatening. Then Eliza thought of Master Crowe, with his tall straight back and his harsh demeanor. Master Crowe always seemed to want to teach Eliza a lesson in morals.

Rules, rules, she thought indignantly. Mama has rules. The Lighthouse Service has rules. Amanda Jane and the pastor have rules, and God only knows the school has rules.

Eliza bit her lip and scowled. Then, all at once, she abruptly threw the *Rules for Teachers* down on the table. "Well, then, I suppose it's lucky for me that halls, barbershops, yacht clubs, restaurants, and saloons are only for men. For that matter, so are the voting booths!" she said hotly.

Sophie looked up at Eliza, startled. When she spoke her voice was firm and even. "Listen to me. No one is asking anything unreasonable of you. Anger will not get you what you desire in life."

Eliza noticed that Sophie's white skin was growing red.

"I thought you desired to teach," Sophie said tersely. "If you don't fancy teaching, tell me right now so that I can tell the principal in the morning."

After a long pause, Eliza spoke. "Please don't go to the principal," she said, more calmly now. "I want the teaching position."

"That's the spirit," said Sophie.

Several days later, Eliza stood at the front of the fourth-grade classroom and wrote her name on the blackboard. She paced about nervously as she waited for her pupils to arrive. How am I ever going to manage a class by myself? she thought. It seemed an impossible task. Still, she was determined to be a success. She brushed some lint off her blue serge skirt and checked her hair to make sure it was securely fastened. Then the first scholar, a tiny girl about nine years old with orange braids and a tightly buttoned brown wool coat, entered the classroom. She hung up her coat at the back of the room, near the potbellied stove. Then she politely made her curtsy to Eliza before taking her seat at one of the desks.

"What's your name?" Eliza asked the child.

"Lizzie," the girl answered shyly. Eliza smiled at her.

More children filed into the classroom and chatted as they hung up their coats and took off their scarves and mittens. To Eliza's alarm, the small rectangular room was full a few minutes later. The children seemed to Eliza like puppies as they all moved about. She counted them: five girls and sixteen boys. She had been told to expect twenty-one children, but no one had told her sixteen of them would be boys! I'm only six or seven years older than these children, Eliza thought. She noticed that some of the boys were so tall that they couldn't fit their long legs under their desks. How am I going to make them mind me? she asked herself.

Sophie dropped in for a quick visit, darting in and out of the room with an elegant swish of black skirts. "Just remember I'm down the hall if you need any help. You'll do fine," she said.

Eliza felt her heart pounding. "My name is Miss Brown," she began. Her voice quivered. Next she told the class to stand for the Pledge of Allegiance, and found, to her horror, that she was so nervous she forgot some of the words. She had barely coaxed the children to their seats and begun the roll call when a loud horn interrupted her. All the children jumped out of their seats and ran to the window at the back corner of the room to watch a ferry from Hart Island pass by. As everyone knew, the ferry to Hart Island carried the unclaimed dead of New York City.

"Please return to your desks," Eliza said, and cleared her throat. Most of the pupils ignored her. Then the door opened and the principal appeared.

"I was just checking on you to make sure these boys were behaving," announced the elfin Hosiah Prim. "The switch is in the corner of the room," he told Eliza, and gave her a wink as the boys who were standing took their seats.

"Thank you, sir," Eliza said, relieved to have the principal's support.

"I appreciate your help over the next few weeks. Of course, there is a possibility that Miss Higgins will not be strong enough to return to school and that I'll need you until June," he said thoughtfully, stroking his goatee.

June? Eliza thought. Would she be able to last for even the next hour? Little Lizzie gave Eliza a sympathetic look, as if she knew what Eliza was thinking.

"All the parents will be coming to the lower school Christmas pageant in another month," the principal continued. "Your class is performing a puppet show of the Wise Men meeting the Christ child. I'm afraid Miss Higgins was not able to begin the preparations before she left, so I think you had best get started writing the script, making the puppets, and building the stage. That is, after your class's regular lessons are over."

Eliza gulped and awkwardly folded her hands together behind her, feeling very small. "We'll begin today," she said with foreboding. She wondered how she was going to manage to direct a production in so short a time.

The rest of the day Eliza frenetically hustled about from desk to desk to sort out disciplinary problems. It was terrible. As one boy was reciting from the McGuffey reader, she caught Justin, who was known as a problem, forcing dead insects into the holes in his desk. In the late morning, Lizzie let out a squeal when Justin attached a leech to her neck. "Justin, go to the corner of the room," Eliza said firmly, and she was amazed when he did so. After the lunch recess, several children came back from Ford's Candy Store with treats, which of course needed to be confiscated.

Then, in the late afternoon, Eliza had her final interruption of the day. While all the other children were figuring sums, she looked over and saw Justin drawing a picture of her on his slate. The picture showed Eliza standing at the front of the room with her hands on her hips and her lips drawn into a straight line. It captured her exactly, Eliza thought with a twinge of annoyance. He'd drawn that determined look Mama was always talking about.

"What's this?" she asked, taking Justin's slate.

Justin smirked, then shifted in his seat apprehensively.

"Wipe that clean, please, and do your sums," Eliza said flatly.

"Are you going to hit me with the switch?" Justin challenged.

"I don't think so. I'd more likely take you to the principal," Eliza replied. She did not want Justin to get the better of her. "Why don't we come to an agreement?" she asked.

Justin's red mouth gaped open, revealing a slight overbite. He said nothing.

"The agreement is," Eliza said, "you help me and I'll help you. How's that? If you behave in class and you help me with a special project, I won't take you down to the principal."

"All right," he answered, bewildered.

"Good," Eliza said, feeling that something, however small, had finally been accomplished. "I think you're a very good artist. How are you at stage design?"

Chapter 12

L iving with Amanda Jane and the pastor is a challenge and a nuisance, Eliza wrote in her sketchbook journal. Beside the words she drew a picture of her bald clerical brother-in-law, smugly reading a book in the parsonage living room.

Eliza put down her pen and looked up when she heard a knock at the door. It was Pastor Lawrence. Eliza quickly shut her sketchbook and slipped it in the drawer of her desk before the pastor entered the room.

Speak of the dickens, she thought. Isn't it just like the pastor to appear when someone's thinking about him?

"Time for supper," Pastor Lawrence said.

"Thank you. I'll be there in a minute."

With the turn of a heel, the pastor left. Eliza was annoyed at his presence in her room. She put the sketchbook underneath her mattress before going into the dining room. The table was already set; that was supposed to be her chore, and she had forgotten. The muffins Eliza had made that morning were put out, but she noticed that Amanda Jane had cut off their burnt bottoms.

"I apologize for not remembering to lay the table and I'm sorry I burnt the muffins," Eliza told her sister apologetically.

Amanda Jane nodded and frowned.

The pastor said the prayer, then cut the chicken. He put a few thin slices onto a plate and passed it to Eliza. Eliza helped herself to potatoes and string beans.

"How was teaching today?" Amanda Jane asked.

"Awful," Eliza replied. "The children broke the handle off the American flag and did a number of other terrible things."

"You must learn discipline," the pastor said. "True caring involves discipline, and we must not forget that."

Amanda Jane said, "I agree." Didn't Amanda Jane always agree with the pastor? Eliza thought, and shrugged. She noticed that the pastor had heaped his plate high with potatoes and that he had given himself a generous serving of chicken as well.

Did discipline always have to be the topic of conversation? she wondered. "Pastor, I'm enjoying the book you gave me," Eliza said, changing the conversation.

"Which book was that?"

The Wizard of Oz."

"An excellent book," he said, licking his fingers. "There's a good story behind it, too. L. Frank Baum couldn't decide what to call the Emerald City. Then he looked across the room at his file cabinets and read *'A–G,'*

'H–N,' and 'O–Z,' so he called the city Oz. This is often the way art happens, wouldn't you agree?"

"Yes, I think so. I appreciate your anecdote, sir," Eliza answered. How complicated her emotions were regarding the pastor. One minute she disliked him intensely, the next she found him engaging, almost winsome. The pastor, like her, loved books, and, like her, he enjoyed reading almost any kind. If only their conversations related exclusively to reading, she mused, they'd be a great deal better off.

"Eliza, as your spiritual advisor . . . ," the pastor started.

"Yes?" Eliza asked, instantly suspicious.

"As your spiritual advisor, I feel that perhaps you should be showing me your journal. You do keep one, I've observed."

Eliza ran her tongue over her teeth, then pressed her lips tightly together. "It's a sketchbook, though sometimes I write a few notes. It's not exactly a journal and no, I won't show it to you."

"When you are ready, then. I won't repeat myself. I will wait until you come to me," the pastor said.

Amanda Jane came to Eliza's defense. "Lawrence, don't make Eliza show you her journal. Perhaps as she gains our trust she will want to. In the meantime, Eliza, I want you to know that both of us are available for your spiritual concerns."

"Thanks," Eliza replied glumly. Then, under her breath, "Why won't you simply leave me alone!"

"What did you say?" the pastor asked.

"Nothing."

Eliza chewed the rest of her dinner in silence. Then she asked to be excused, letting Amanda Jane know she would be back to help clear the dishes. She was lying on her bed, facedown, when her sister entered her bedroom.

"What do you want?" Eliza asked crossly.

"Turn around and face me, young lady. Sit up, please."

Eliza sat up and looked at her sister, who was now noticeably heavier because of her pregnancy. Amanda Jane's neck and jaw looked rigid with tension.

"Listen to me," Amanda Jane began. "What you did just now was uncalled-for and rude. While you are living in this household, I expect you to be courteous, cheerful, and polite—not stubborn and self-centered. Lawrence has been exceedingly generous toward you. At the very least you could act respectfully toward him."

"Yes, I can do that," Eliza answered, "but I will never give him my journal."

"As you wish."

Eliza paused for a moment, then said, "Amanda Jane, I don't want to go out in the evenings with you and the pastor anymore. May I stay home by myself?"

Amanda Jane sighed. "Being a part of this household means doing the things that a pastor does. As the minister he is obliged to attend a great many social events. If he asks us to accompany him, we are to do so graciously."

"I don't wish to," Eliza said.

Amanda Jane continued, "Haven't you had the opportunity to eat on fine china? Haven't you had more opportunities in the last month than you've had in your entire lifetime?"

Eliza thought of the *Saturday Evening Post* and *Harper's*

magazines that the pastor had given her and felt guilty for not appreciating him more than she did. What her sister had said was quite true.

"I'm sorry, Amanda Jane. I will do better."

"All right, then," her sister said, looking relieved. "If I were you I'd look my best for the taffy pull tonight. You'll be wearing your Sunday blouse, won't you? You'd better iron it, and don't forget to mend that small tear on the shoulder."

After her sister left the room, Eliza made faces at her. The very idea of it—sharing her private book with the pastor! It was a good thing she'd been hiding the book all along. She went to her desk and took out paper, pen, and inkwell. For a moment she entertained the idea of keeping two journals, a real one and a fraudulent one for Pastor Lawrence. She tested her pen on the paper by making a few zigzags, then wrote:

Saturday, November 21.   Woke early. Read the Sermon on the Mount and reviewed its godly messages. Helped with breakfast and the washing up. Went to school and rehearsed the Christmas pageant with the children. Found disciplining some of the boys necessary when they broke the chalk, two slates, and the flag. Read book in the evening. Prayers and bedtime.

"Eliza C. Brown, you should be ashamed!" she said out loud. Deciding she would not keep a fake journal, she crumpled the paper into a ball. Then she threw it in the wastebasket.

_____

That evening, Sophie arrived at the church hall early to help set up the tables. One of Eliza's duties was to keep the drawers in the church hall's kitchen orderly. When she and Sophie opened the drawers, Eliza was embarrassed to see she had not folded the tablecloths very well. This was exactly the sort of thing the old ladies of the church, the ones who kept their flower-arranging supplies in those drawers, would be sure to report to the pastor. Sophie quietly helped Eliza tidy up the drawers without saying anything about the mess.

Eliza poured cider into glasses while Sophie set up tables and put out molasses, sugar, vinegar, butter, and other ingredients that they'd be using to make the candy. Eliza was about to complain to her about the pastor but decided instead to hold her tongue. Sophie seemed sad; it looked as though she had been crying. Eliza knew she must be thinking of Peter.

"I've just come to help you, Eliza. I'm not going to stay."

"I understand," Eliza replied. "You're wishing Peter were here."

Sophie nodded, and sniffled.

"I miss him terribly," Eliza said. Then she ventured, "You're a very brave person, Sophie. First you lost your husband and now you've lost Peter. I don't know how you've managed."

"We all have our folders of things we are intended to do in this life. It's just that some of us have thicker folders than others. All this pain hasn't made me any better than the next person, but it *has* given me a certain intuition," Sophie said with a sigh.

Then, as they finished laying the tables, the conversation turned again to Peter. He had been an awkward guest at parties. Poor Peter! Eliza thought. It must have terrified him to have a girlfriend like Sophie, who was not only extremely attractive and very sophisticated, but who came with a pack of gregarious aunts, uncles, and cousins from a prominent family on the Island.

"I never saw Peter at many parties, but I can imagine he was terrible in trying to make conversation with new people," Eliza said. "I'm very awkward myself. I have very few social graces."

"There's very little to learn. Besides, I don't think you've missed out on much."

"How can you say that!" Eliza said. "You must have been to many concerts and dances and other exciting events."

Sophie told Eliza that while her life in New York City had been a constant whirl of social events, she had also had to submit to her husband and in-laws, as well as her parents and grandparents. The slow pace of life on City Island was what had attracted her to the place. She'd visited her great-aunt Delia and great-uncle Stephen's house often when she was a little girl, and she'd always remembered the wide and lovely expanse of lawn that sloped down to the water, and her great-aunt's beautiful garden on the hill. There were always children playing on the lawn and usually a dog or two racing about. She remembered her uncles, the marine pilots, leaning against the seawalls, drinking and smoking cigars, and she remembered how excited everyone would become when they'd see a big ship on the horizon.

"Peter was part of this magical existence that was so different from my own. He was kind and humble and he lived a simple life," Sophie told Eliza. Eliza was touched that Sophie had loved her brother so deeply.

Amanda Jane and a few women from the parish, their arms full of packages, entered the hall, and Amanda Jane escorted them to the kitchen. Eliza was relieved that Amanda Jane would take over the taffy making, since she herself tended to overcook taffy and give it a burnt flavor. Charles Boxley then came into the room, looking dandy in a new checkered suit and matching hat, which was slightly flattened on top. Figures he'd show up, Eliza thought.

"Here comes one of your admirers," Sophie said.

"Everywhere I go, that Charles Boxley seems to appear," Eliza whispered back. "Isn't it convenient for him that I've now moved to the Island?"

Charles seemed in good spirits as he happily chewed something in the corner of his mouth. "I have something to show you two ladies," he said. "A new invention from Manhattan: Blibber Blubber."

"Blibber Blubber?"

"Here, try it," Charles said, and offered Eliza a long, flat, gray stick. "I predict all the children on the Island will soon know about this and that there will be no end to it."

"This is against my better judgment," Eliza said as she put the stick into her mouth. It was a soft food with a strange, bland flavor. Eliza made a face and Sophie giggled.

"Don't swallow it," Charles instructed.

Just as he was saying this, Eliza swallowed the Blibber Blubber. It soon felt like a small, round pebble in her stomach.

"I told you not to swallow," Charles said.

"Blibber Blubber," Sophie said with a laugh. "Now what do you do with it?"

Charles blew a bubble and made Sophie laugh again. Then Eliza laughed. She laughed so hard her stomach hurt and tears welled up in her eyes.

Sophie and Eliza finished setting up the tables; then Sophie excused herself to go home. "I'm not ready to be social, but you have a lovely time," she told Eliza, and gave her a quick kiss on the forehead.

Soon the church hall had filled with people of all ages. The pastor came after a while and he and Amanda Jane started to greet the visitors. Then several churchwomen carried a big pot out from the kitchen and slowly poured the sticky brown syrup onto a buttered platter. The taffy was still too hot to handle.

Charles followed Eliza from table to table as she served the cider. Then Alfred appeared, wearing a clean white shirt and a new bow tie. He looked good, but his bangs were cut too short. The expression on his face seemed very serious.

"Want some cider?" Eliza asked nonchalantly.

"No, thanks. May I have a word with you?"

Alfred took her aside to the back of the kitchen, away from the women and the large pots of taffy. He frowned.

"What's the matter?" Eliza said.

"I want to say . . . you being new to the Island and not knowing many people and especially being in such a vulnerable state after the tragedy that has transpired as of late . . . well, I want you to know I intend to look after you. This is exactly the time when young girls fall prey to all sorts of devilments."

"Devilments?" Eliza repeated.

"People who take advantage. Men, to be specific."

"Don't be silly!" she said. "What kind of danger am I likely to run into at a taffy pull?"

"As you like, then. Let me leave it at this: I want you to feel free to call on me anytime," Alfred said knowingly. If he didn't insist on always telling her what was best, Eliza imagined, she would favor him much more.

Alfred combed his straight brown hair with his fingers and said, "All I ever intend is to help you and to point you in the right direction. I wish you wouldn't push me away."

"Why does everyone think I'm so helpless?" Eliza demanded. "Please don't worry about me so much," she said, ending the conversation. Then she followed Alfred into the hall and let him give her a lesson in candy pulling, leaving people to serve their own cider.

Alfred began to form the syrup into a mass, working it with a spoon. "When you gather up the taffy, start pulling it with your fingertips. Then fold it back on itself like this. Now twist while you fold and pull," he told her. Eliza watched Alfred transform the sticky mass into a glistening ribbon. "Got it? Now we'll do a big piece together. Do you think you're strong enough to pull it with your hands or do you need to use a candy hook?"

"I've done this before," Eliza said, annoyed. She soon found she was enjoying herself, however, as she and

Alfred pulled a big lump of the hot taffy until they'd created an elastic rope a few feet in length. When the taffy began to hold its shape, they brought it to the kitchen counter to cut it with scissors.

"It's good," Eliza said as she ate a piece of the candy. Then Charles pushed his way in. How tedious, she thought; she was stuck with Charles again! Alfred had now worked his way through the crowd to the other side of the room and was pulling taffy with Carlotta Proudfit, one of their classmates, showing off his fancier folds and twists.

Eliza found Charles a less skillful and enthusiastic partner than Alfred. His grip didn't seem as firm as Alfred's, and he seemed weak and soft all over, like the taffy or the Blibber Blubber. But his manner was far more tolerant than Alfred's. She liked him a little, maybe.

Having pulled candy for about half an hour, Eliza and Charles washed their hands and walked outside. "Here, have my jacket," he said.

Charles stood against the thick trunk of the big oak tree near the fence. Something about him seems a little wormy, Eliza thought, yet he's kind and easygoing. She took a step toward him. "There's the Pleiades," she said.

"How do you know about the stars?" Charles asked. She was conscious of his moving closer to her now. He put his hands on her shoulders for a few minutes. It felt nice, she thought, and pretended nothing was unusual.

"My papa told me about the stars," she said. "Peter knew how to navigate by them; I can too, a little."

Eliza arched her back and pointed with one arm. "There," she said. "Betelgeuse, the red star, in Orion.

110

There's Orion's belt with the three stars hanging. The middle one's the Orion nebula."

"You're very intelligent and you're very beautiful," Charles said.

"Thank you," she answered. Charles drew her closer to him and she looked into his eyes, anxiously waiting, and studying the lines on his forehead. A kiss, that's what he wanted. She wished she didn't dislike the smell of his hair tonic so much.

Charles leaned toward Eliza and kissed her. Eliza drew back, shocked. His lips were wet, and she didn't like the experience at all! She hoped Charles would not want to kiss her again, but she could tell he already wanted to.

Eliza examined Charles's mouse-colored hair and ran it through her fingers. His curls, stiff and flat, were a little greasy to the touch. She took off his glasses and felt his face, his mustache, and his lips. His lips were well formed and he had perfect teeth. Then she felt the rough sides of his face and his chin. He was smiling contentedly and seemed pleased that she was touching him.

"Do you want me to grow a beard?" Charles asked.

"No," Eliza answered flatly.

Charles took Eliza's hand. His was a pale, slim hand, she considered, similar to her own. He leaned over to kiss her again.

"I'm going inside now," she said.

That night at the parsonage, thinking a lot about Peter and a little about Charles Boxley, Eliza couldn't sleep. She got up and went to the bathroom, and on her way back to her room she could hear Amanda Jane and the pastor talking. She tried not to listen, until she realized they were discussing her.

"I agree with you, my dear," Pastor Lawrence said. "Our girl is indeed becoming more stubborn and unruly. She is growing far too independent! She is a good girl, however."

"Eliza's unkempt-looking," Amanda Jane pointed out, "and I worry that she reads too much. Her passions are easily excited."

"Well, she eats and sleeps, and that is a favorable sign that it is not a mental malady."

Thank God for that, Eliza said to herself angrily.

"This is the nature of the soul," the pastor said. "Your sister is undergoing great changes, and in such times it is a natural thing for one to want to be left alone. Perhaps if she doesn't want to spend time with us she shouldn't be made to. The girl has made many friends on the Island in this short time, and that again is a good sign."

"Mama and I have been talking. What *sorts* of friends is Eliza acquiring?"

With this the pastor laughed, then answered, "You are thinking of Sophie Long. Is that who you are worried about, my dear?"

"Yes," said Amanda Jane. "In Sophie, Eliza has found a way to bask in her grief, and she may never come out of it. Furthermore, women such as Sophie who keep to themselves and never join any of the ladies' societies become very strange. Is this the company my sister ought to have? Often I have questioned whether or not I ought to be letting Eliza go over to her place."

"Intelligent women on their own. Yes, these are the

ones who have conflicts and go insane. I have seen it often, Amanda Jane. Though I wonder, whose job is it to say what is right or wrong in the eyes of God? But Sophie has the glow which radiates the Spirit. Eliza is keeping good company. You needn't worry," the pastor said.

With that, Eliza had heard all she wanted to hear and returned to her room.

Chapter 13

"Teacher, help me paint the angel's wings. Do angels have colors in their wings?"

"You could have a little pink and a little blue, Lizzie. Perhaps angels have wings like birds," Eliza said. "I'd make the colors very subtle, like shadows."

"What does *subtle* mean?"

"Inconspicuous."

"What does *inconspicuous* mean?"

"Indistinct, not standing out too much. Yet at the same time angels are dazzling and magnificent. However you paint the wings will be fine, Lizzie."

Lizzie proudly held up her angel puppet for Eliza to see. It was a small, crudely sewn rag doll with a purple dress, cardboard wings, and a painted face supported by a thin garden stake. Some of the sticks the children were using to hold their puppets had previously been used to hold up Sophie's tomato plants.

"Very, very nice," Eliza said, amused that some of the girls had chosen to clothe their angels in purple.

"We don't have any more white paint, Teacher. Can I use paste?" Lizzie asked.

"Go ahead, use paste. You can mix it on this piece of cardboard."

Eliza helped the little girls mix the flour and water for the paste. Keeping these children occupied was certainly a challenge, she thought, though she realized she was now enjoying herself. She had decided to conduct the fourth-grade class exactly the way she would have liked it if she had been a fourth-grader. "Make sure the paste stays on the cardboard," Eliza warned.

The whole classroom had been converted into a work-room to make puppets and props for the Christmas pageant. At one corner of the room, the girls made the winged angel puppets, and in another some of the boys painted the big wooden puppet stage that Eliza and Sophie had constructed. In other areas of the room, boys were creating the Three Wise Men, using feathers and beads for their treasures. Other boys were putting together a motley-looking Mary, Joseph, and Jesus out of scraps of material from Amanda Jane's sewing collection. The rest of the boys were fashioning the shepherds and animals of the manger from pieces of cardboard. Everything seemed to be going well for the moment—as long as Eliza could keep pace with them.

"Felix, bring the scissors over to Teddy. Christine, please don't stand on the chair! Justin, come down from there!" Eliza said, and raced to the corner of the room where Justin was standing unsteadily on tiptoe on one of the desktops as he painted the stage.

The stage had one large, square central panel where

Justin had rendered the town of Bethlehem with straight, square two-story buildings, similar to those of City Island, plus a barn and a winding road, against a starry backdrop of bright cobalt blue. The deep blue sky continued high up on the triangular pediment. There at the very top of the triangle, Justin was straining to paint Bethlehem's single bright star, the Star of Wonder.

"I can't reach the top of the stage to paint it. I'm going to fetch the stepladder," Justin said, ignoring Eliza completely. Before Eliza could stop him, the boy ran out of the room and slammed the door. She dared not leave the classroom unattended.

"Justin, wait!" she said, but it was too late.

Eliza turned to see the girls still mixing paste on the cardboard. They had poured so much water onto the board that it had run over the sides, and white pools were forming on one of the desks.

"Sorry, Teacher," Lizzie said.

"It wasn't me who did it," another little girl said.

"Oh, fiddlesticks!" Eliza exclaimed with an exasperated sigh. "We need to find some rags to clean this up. I wonder where rags are kept in this school." The little devils, she thought. Five girls and sixteen boys. I almost wish I hadn't left the lighthouse, where there was at least some peace and quiet.

Just then, a tall, imposing form appeared at the door of the classroom. It was Master Crowe, holding Justin firmly by the arm. Justin looked as if he was about to cry. Master Crowe knit his brows as he witnessed the activity in Eliza's classroom, and Eliza felt the old, familiar dread she'd always experienced with him. After the teacher released Justin, he took Eliza aside for a private meeting in the hallway.

"Miss, I have just found this boy running up and down every hall in this school. Do not let it happen again. May I ask exactly what is going on here?"

"W-We are preparing for the pageant," Eliza stammered, hoping Master Crowe would comment favorably on the impressive stage Justin had painted.

"It looks as though you're making a mess."

"Is it a crime, sir, for students to enjoy themselves in school?"

"At the expense of your class's lessons?"

"In addition, sir."

"If you do not learn to better discipline your students, I will see to it that your every action is supervised. I can assure you, Miss Brown, the principal is going to hear of your escapades."

Master Crowe doesn't like me and perhaps he'll persuade the principal not to like me either. I have a terrible feeling everything's going to go wrong today, Eliza worried as she woke up on the day of the pageant. She was seventeen today, and in the frenzy of the past few weeks, she'd almost forgotten her birthday. She parted the linen curtains over her window and was delighted to see that snow had fallen in the night, lightly covering the Island. Plump brown sparrows hopped on the snow-covered lawn, pecking at the seeds that Amanda Jane had put out for them. How quickly life can change from day to day, Eliza mused. Time passes and I hardly recognize myself.

At the City Island School, the fourth-grade play was

one of a number of festivities in the assembly room that day, including a piano concert and singers. Eliza panicked when she noticed Master Crowe and the principal sitting together in the front row. The parents of the children were there, and many of the townsfolk as well.

When it was time for her class's presentation, Eliza, Sophie, and some of the larger, stronger children moved the huge three-sided puppet stage from the back of the assembly room. Since the front was heavier than the shorter sides, the stage wobbled precariously and fell thundering to the floor with a loud crash. I knew something like this would happen, Eliza thought with dread. But trusty Alfred appeared from the audience and helped put the stage back up. She thanked him profusely.

Eliza extinguished the lights, except for the small candle lanterns they set up in front of the proscenium. Behind the red velvet curtain, on the stage's platform, she sat in the darkness with the five girls and sixteen boys. "Try to move the puppets gently across, not wildly. Hold your rods as still as you can. Justin, see if you can untangle those angels," Eliza whispered.

"I'm nervous," Lizzie said, and hugged Eliza.

"I am, too," Eliza said. Truly, she seemed more nervous than the children.

The Christmas story began with the crudely drawn sheep, camel, and shepherd puppets stiffly moving along on rods in a line from one side of the stage to the other, bouncing up and down. Each of the flat painted cardboard animals had two identical sides, a front and a back, sandwiched over a rod. The problem with the animals, Eliza noticed, was that some were much larger than others. One sheep was nearly twice as large as the camel. A few, like the lion and the bear, probably didn't belong in Bethlehem at all. Eliza wondered what the principal was going to think about Joseph and Mary in their wildly colored patchwork robes and long hair of yarn. Then she whispered to the children to remember to crouch down in back of the stage so that their heads would not be seen by the audience.

Oh, I give up worrying about this, Eliza thought as she nervously ran her fingers through her hair. I'll just let everything happen as it will happen. A tiny boy with a neat tweed jacket and dark tie read the narrator's role, boldly and clearly: " '. . . And lo, the star, which they saw in the east, went before them, till it came and stood over where the young child was. When they saw the star, they rejoiced with exceeding great joy.' "

Eliza sat back to watch the children putting on the play. All of a sudden, by some miracle, it seemed to her that the children's voices were actually those of Mary and Joseph. Soon the tiny baby Jesus was born and the five purple angels descended in glory. The odd menagerie of animals—sheep, bear, goats, camel, lion, and tiger—crowded around the manger with the shepherds, and the three turbaned Wise Men came in one by one, offering their treasures. All the colorful puppets on sticks against the starry sky of Bethlehem suddenly seemed to Eliza to be extraordinarily beautiful and, peering around the side of the stage to watch the presentation, she found herself moved.

"That was fun!" one of the boys said to another when the play was over. Eliza realized with surprise that none of the many boys in her class had argued or wrestled the entire afternoon.

"You all did a wonderful job," Eliza whispered to the children.

"They liked the stage, didn't they?" Justin eagerly asked Eliza.

"Yes, everyone loved the stage, especially me," she said, and patted Justin on the head. Justin had painted nearly the whole stage himself, with only a tiny bit of guidance from Eliza.

Eliza lit the lamps in the room and the children came out from behind the stage, one by one, with their puppets. She turned toward Master Crowe and watched the furrows in his brow soften. He was pleased with the performance, she saw with great relief. Then the principal, Mr. Hosiah Prim, called Eliza by name, and said proudly as she stood in front of the audience, "Here is the director of this excellent presentation."

Against a backdrop of enthusiastic clapping and cheering, Eliza looked from one face to another in the crowd: Pastor Lawrence with her very pregnant-looking sister, Sophie and Jenny, Alfred, Charles Boxley, and Sophie's great-aunt Delia. There were many other people, too, whom Eliza recognized. By now she knew most of the parents of the children in her class, and most people in the church parish as well. She realized she had many more friends than she had ever believed she would have, and this made her feel joyful.

Justin's parents introduced themselves to Eliza at the coffee hour and thanked her for the attention she'd given

120

their son. Then Sophie caught Eliza's arm and the two friends embraced.

"Are you all right, Eliza, my dear? You look as if you were about to cry."

Eliza brushed the tears away from her eyes and wiped her hands on her brown skirt. "It's these children . . . and everyone. I don't despise them so very much anymore, Sophie."

"You did a beautiful job with the pageant. I hope you are happy with yourself also?"

"I am," Eliza answered shyly.

Sophie took out a brown paper package from her bag of schoolbooks and handed it to Eliza. "Happy birthday," she said.

Eliza unwrapped the bundle and let the red ribbons fall to the floor. Her present was a deep purple, low-necked organdy dress with puffed sleeves. "I'm touched that you made me a dress. I don't know when you found the time. You've kept it such a secret!"

"I worked on the dress in the evenings after you'd gone home. It was no trouble. Do you like it?"

Eliza unfolded the dress and held it against herself. It fell to just above her ankles, in the latest style, which so far on the Island only Sophie had dared to wear. "Oh, Sophie. It's beautiful. I love it," she said. "It's the best present I've ever received."

Something lost, something gained, Eliza said to herself. Hers had been an awful, terrible loss, and it always would be. Yet she'd gained more in the past few months than she could have imagined.

Eliza wore her new dress on Christmas Day, when Mama and Sam came over from the lighthouse for the service and a formal noonday dinner at the parsonage. Sundays were just about the only time Eliza saw Mama now, and she hadn't seen Papa in weeks. Sometimes she missed her parents, and then again she often did not. She even found herself missing Sam occasionally. Seeing Mama across the table now, so silent and removed, she thought of the many chores that she must now be doing, alone, in anticipation of another visit by the inspector. She wanted to tell Mama about her new life, how full and joyful it had become, but she didn't know what to say.

"What's happening at the lighthouse, Mama?"

"It's quiet without you. We do our chores. Sam has rearranged his room. He took Peter's charts off the wall. One of Peter's friends, that scruffy fellow, Ralph, stopped by to pay his respects one day and I gave him the charts."

"You gave away the charts, Mama? How could you? We'll never see those charts again!" Eliza was hurt and angry. Anything of Peter's was precious to her. Somehow it seemed that if Peter's room at the lighthouse was kept just the way it was, then it wouldn't hurt so much to have to go into it—maybe then for a split second it would be possible to pretend he wasn't dead.

"Don't frown so, daughter. Your father has many, many charts, and remember this: Peter's things cannot be kept together for eternity," Mama said in her Irish brogue.

"I wish you had asked me first. I wish you had kept the charts."

"Never you mind, Eliza. For shame! You know our Peter would not have us treat his room like a mausoleum."

"Besides, it's my room," Sam put in.

"Your room *is* a mausoleum," Eliza said sarcastically. Sam's macabre collection had probably taken over the whole space, she thought with disgust. What other poor creatures had Sam captured and collected since she had last seen his room? She was glad she no longer had occasion to see the changes going on in the lighthouse.

"Mama, you haven't given away Peter's ship models, have you?"

"I would never do that. Not for the world," Mama said.

Eliza was relieved to be able to cut the time with her family short to go to see Charles in his mother's fine house, where she had been invited for tea by Mrs. Boxley. Charles and his mother lived in what had once been a colonial tavern, and Eliza looked forward to seeing it. But she was suspicious of Charles's intentions in making the invitation. She knew his tall, elegant, white-haired mother—a widow whose husband had been run over by a trolley in Manhattan many years back—from Trinity Church. Being formally invited to her house was another matter, particularly on Christmas Day.

In a large, comfortable parlor, Mrs. Boxley's Irish servant girl, Edna, served a fancy round pound cake that had an intricate floral design on it made from powdered sugar.

How pleasant this is! Eliza thought to herself as she took her piece of cake. She looked around the room, and her gaze came to rest on a series of pewter plates and measuring mugs on the carved mantelpiece above the fireplace. Nearby, on a small oak side table next to the sofa, were Charles's recent newspaper clippings. Charles had taken a special interest in the Wright brothers' first flight over the sand dunes of Kitty Hawk, North Carolina.

Eliza sipped her tasty orange-flavored tea. She had never had a drink like it before. From across the table, Charles eyed her warmly. He seemed a nice man, it was true, though she still couldn't make up her mind how she felt about him.

"Eliza directed the puppet show at the school's Christmas pageant," Charles told his mother.

"That's a big responsibility for a young lady," Mrs. Boxley stated.

"Yes, it was!" Eliza responded.

"You'll be teaching school until June, Eliza?" Charles asked her.

"Yes, it looks that way," Eliza said. "Miss Higgins still has pneumonia. I never dreamed I'd be put in charge for so long."

"The assignment obviously came to you at a good time—when you needed to occupy yourself and put yourself back into the stream of life," Mrs. Boxley said kindly.

"Absolutely," Eliza replied. She tried to remember to chew her food with her mouth closed. Amanda Jane had pointed out to her that she sometimes made smacking sounds with her lips and didn't always close her mouth when she ate.

"After June, what will you do?" Charles asked. "Will you continue to teach at the school?"

"I think so," Eliza answered happily. Since the pageant, she'd felt fairly sure she would be asked to stay on at the school. But she couldn't be certain. She'd probably continue to live in the parsonage. But she couldn't be certain of that either! Amanda Jane would have her baby in late March or early April. In June, Eliza would graduate from school. Would Amanda and the pastor still want her to live with them once the baby was born? Or would everyone expect her to go back to the lighthouse?

After tea, Eliza and Charles put their coats on to take a walk in the Boxleys' snow-covered garden. Charles carried his camera equipment under his arm.

"I want to show you something," he said.

In the garden, on a lone vine growing against the garden shed, was a single red rose.

"A rose, blooming in winter!" Eliza said, surprised. She took in the sight as she always did when she came upon something beautiful.

Charles set up his tripod, mounted his heavy square camera on it, and disappeared for a few minutes underneath the soiled camera skirt. Then, *poof!* Eliza stepped back in alarm at the sound of the explosion.

"I'd forgotten cameras were so loud," she said.

"That's the flash. This is just about the most modern camera sold," Charles said proudly. "Maybe in the springtime I'll buy the new model."

Charles is an artist, just like me! Eliza realized. But as Charles took one picture after another, she began to grow cold and impatient. She crossed her arms and wrapped her scarf around her head. How many pictures can a man take of one flower? she wondered.

He's not paying the least bit of attention to me, she said to herself a moment later. Here I am in my new Sunday dress with my nice coat and pin and my favorite green woven scarf. I look pretty. Why isn't this man taking *my* picture?

Charles continued fiddling and experimenting, moving the tripod around to photograph the rose from different angles. "It's difficult to find just the right composition," he said.

He's a fool! Eliza told herself. She paced around, trying to keep warm and pretend she was having a good time.

Charles snapped another photograph. *Poof!*

"I'm feeling the chill. Perhaps I'll go inside soon," Eliza commented at last.

Charles put another plate into the camera. Eliza laughed, seeing the humor in the situation now. And I was just about to like him more, she mused. The man's so caught up in his new contraption, he doesn't know an opportunity when he sees one.

"Why are you laughing?" Charles asked.

Because you're an idiot, Eliza thought. Because you're a meticulous man who wears hair tonic and because you're obsessed with taking pictures of that flower and you're just very, very silly. Then she said out loud, "For no reason."

Charles emerged from underneath the camera blanket. "Would you like me to take your picture?" he asked.

"Thank you," Eliza answered. Maybe he's not quite so big a fool as I thought, she said to herself.

She positioned her hair to fall over one shoulder and smiled a genuine smile as Charles took her picture.

126

"I'm receiving my law degree this spring, and then I'll officially become partners with my uncle here on the Island."

"Yes?" she said.

"Well, and I was thinking, we could become engaged then. If you wanted to . . ."

Eliza's heart stopped. She had known Charles for such a short time, yet here he was making her the most serious offer a man could make a woman. She could hardly believe what she was hearing. "To be married? Oh, I don't know!" She blushed.

"Think about it, will you?"

Eliza said, "I'll think about it."

Chapter 14

March 1904

Eliza rose from her bed; she could not sleep. She thought about Charles's proposal of a few months ago. "I'm not ready," she had told him a few days later. What would she say if Charles ever asked her again? The night was still, warm for the early springtime. Through her window, the full moon was rising over the trees, surrounded by a bright orange halo. The house was so quiet that Eliza could hear, in the next room over, the pastor's long, muffled snores, and beyond, in the living room, the gentle ticking of the grandfather clock. She guessed it was around midnight. All at once she had the desire to see her old home, the lighthouse. She quickly dressed herself and threw on her coat. Wrapping her head in her scarf, she stepped outside into the mist.

The rain had stopped and was hanging in the air. Eliza thought she might rummage through the shed in the darkness to find the bicycle, but decided instead to walk the mile to the end of the Island. The dark, bare trees stood out against the fog, dripping beads of water down their branches and onto the ground. The wet gravel of the road glistened. All was quiet on the Island except at the Bucket of Blood Saloon, which was bursting with the chaotic sounds of laughing, loud talking, and ragtime music. Out of habit, Eliza walked slowly past the saloon's dark windows and peered inside.

She thought of Peter's old room in the boardinghouse above the saloon, and for a second she half-expected to see her brother. Five months had gone by since he had died, yet she found that she still looked for him in a crowd, or sitting on a stoop of a storefront, talking to one of his companions from the boatyard.

Eliza quickened her pace and made her way to the landing dock at Belden Point. Straight ahead, the red light of Stepping Stones Lighthouse glowed, a luminous circle in the blue mist high above the water. Eliza had rarely seen the Sound so calm; the beauty of the night made her happy and sad at the same time. Peter, she said to herself, why is it, whenever I see something beautiful, I always think of you?

"How do you do?" a deep, cheerful voice called out. Startled, Eliza turned to see a man close behind her, leaning against the picket fence that ran along the street. It was Ralph. Had she walked by him before and not noticed him? she wondered. Ralph held a garter snake in his hands. "How do you do?" he repeated.

"Fine," Eliza said. She took a tentative step closer. She hadn't seen Ralph since that awful day when everyone in the town had gathered in the parsonage. She studied Ralph's well-sculpted face—his full mustache; straight, shoulder-length black hair; and long straight nose that was set just a bit crookedly on his face. Ralph's build was lean and strong. From his belt hung a dagger in a leather case. He's a wild man, Eliza thought, but he seems a happy, buoyant character.

"Where are you walking?" Ralph asked.

"Nowhere. I'm just walking," Eliza said. She felt herself smiling bashfully.

"You're missing Peter tonight and you've gone down to the water to talk to him," Ralph said.

"Yes. How did you know?"

"I talk to him all the time myself. Especially when I'm fishing. I drink some beer, then I pour a little in the water for Peter and I say, 'Go catch a big one for me, buddy.' He hears us when we talk to him."

"I suppose," Eliza said. "Let me see the snake."

Ralph gently held the snake by its middle and passed it to Eliza. She held it as it writhed in her hands. She was not afraid of it.

Ralph explained that he'd needed to remove the snake from the street before someone could come along in a carriage and crush it. Then he said, "Come with me; we'll set him free in the grass."

Eliza wondered whether or not she should accompany this wild man, but she could see no danger. In the pale moonlight, she followed Ralph up Main Street, past Horton's Store, then off Main Street, behind some houses, around someone's yard, and across another yard. This man certainly seems to know the Island's shortcuts! Eliza remarked to herself as Ralph led her around more houses, through a wooded area, then out to a small open field.

"This is a good place for him, don't you think?" Ralph said, looking around.

"Yes."

"It must be his home." The man talked to the snake tenderly as he bent down to the ground and let it slide from his hands. "Here you are. Now go to your family and friends. There are young ones waiting for you, aren't there?" In another minute, the snake had vanished into the tall, wet brush.

"You have a way with animals, don't you?" Eliza said.

Ralph seemed surprised at her words. "Perhaps," he said, then added, "What should we do now? I've some fishing poles hidden not far from here, in the brush."

"It's late. I need to go home," Eliza said. She could imagine what Amanda Jane and the pastor might do if they knew she was keeping company with Ralph.

"Can I see you tomorrow?"

"I'll be at school."

"After school?"

"I go to my friend Sophie's house to finish my lessons. Then I go home—my sister's home—to do my chores."

"If you ever want to find me, you can go to the docks on the other side of this field," Ralph said, pointing toward the water.

"Is that where you live?"

"Generally."

"The people from town say you're a wild man from the woods," Eliza ventured.

"Is that what they say?" Ralph seemed pleased at this assessment. "What do *you* think?"

"I don't know," she answered honestly.

Ralph laughed hoarsely, and Eliza turned away.

"You're afraid of me," he said.

"No I'm not!" she countered. She *was* a little afraid, though, even if Ralph had been a friend of Peter's. But the unnerving thing was that she was enjoying the company of this wild man. She had better return to the parsonage right away! she told herself. She looked up into the sky. More than an hour had passed since she had left the parsonage; the full moon was now high in the sky.

"Good-bye," she said.

"Are you going to come back and visit me?"

"Perhaps," she answered. "I don't know."

Chapter 15

"How's your balance?" Ralph asked.

"Good, I think," Eliza replied.

With the late-afternoon sun on her back, Eliza followed Ralph across the field, through another hole in a fence, and down a steep hill that opened to the water. The low tide revealed a cluttered beach, a junkyard of sorts: old boat wrecks, a broken crane for hauling boats, giant nails and other sharp objects, railway tracks that were half underwater, and above them, a series of abandoned docks that seemed to have once been part of a shipbuilding center.

"Watch yourself," Ralph said as they darted through the rocks and wreckage on the beach.

The next thing Eliza knew, Ralph had brought her to a place where there was long plank rising up about fifteen feet, connecting the beach to the dock above. The plank was wide but steep and slimy. Still, Ralph ran right up it without hesitation.

"Follow me," he called down.

Eliza lingered, biting her lip a little. So this was why Ralph had asked how her balance was! Would she slip on the plank and fall to her death? Maybe she should put an end to this adventure right now.

Ralph sauntered down the plank and offered her his hand. "It's easy," he said. He told her to put one foot in front of the other and concentrate on the plank as he guided her up. Underneath them, sharp rocks and an old wreck of a carriage jutted out from the beach.

Ralph jumped onto the dock and helped Eliza up too. She breathed a sigh of relief, then noticed the great number of missing boards in the dock. Where there was a gap of three or four boards, she took Ralph's hand as she leapt across.

At the end of the dock, Eliza found pilings, a stack of lumber, and a shed, which contained more abandoned machinery. She sat down on the lumber, a few feet away from Ralph. The view was spectacular from this place: High above the ground, a large part of the Island's shoreline came into view. They could also see the surrounding islands, including the irregular purple tree line of spooky Hart Island. A schooner passed by, its sails going up for its voyage north.

"What do you think of this place?" Ralph asked.

"It's beautiful!" Eliza said.

"Sometimes I wish I could paint. I'd like to paint the reflection of the sun on the water, just as it looks today."

"I paint pictures!" Eliza volunteered. Here was a man with whom, oddly enough, she had something in common.

Ralph pointed to three canoes that were tied together

on the beach—his canoes, he said. Then he pointed to an old workboat mounted on a bluff. "It's gutted out," he told her. "Where there were seats and a ship's wheel, I've hung my hammock."

"Don't you get cold there?"

"I've blankets. Sometimes I stay in a room in town; sometimes I sleep in the woods on Hunter Island and build a bonfire. It's warmest in the woods." Ralph paused and turned his head sharply to the right, then to the left, looking about suspiciously. "Shhh!" he said. "I hear someone."

"Where?" Eliza asked, but Ralph just shushed her again. Then, a few minutes later, two men walking along the beach passed underneath the docks. Eliza was surprised Ralph had sensed the men from so far away.

"It's all right. I think we're safe." Ralph pointed to a small skiff moored out in the water, between the docks and Hart Island. "If I see anyone try to touch my boat," he said with a wild look in his eyes, "I'll put my dagger between my teeth and dive in after them!" Then he added, "What's the matter?"

"It frightens me to hear that kind of talk."

"I'll never hurt *you*," Ralph said. "Go ahead, take a look at my dagger. I know you're curious about it," he said, handing her the knife. "I use it on fish and animals, and hardly ever on people."

Eliza ran her finger lightly along the blade and handed the knife back to Ralph. He laughed a raspy-sounding guffaw, the laugh of someone who was quite possibly in the habit of smoking tobacco.

"You look cold. I'll be right back," he said. He stood

up and went to the shed, then returned with a thick sweater that seemed to Eliza surprisingly well knitted and well cared for.

"This sweater's oiled wool. The Irish make sweaters like this," she said.

"My mother made it. She was Irish," Ralph offered proudly.

Eliza took off her coat, put the sweater on, then put her coat on again. Everything about this man is a mystery, she thought. But why not? Even a wild man who lived in the woods and on abandoned boats could have had a mother who makes sweaters, she figured. She noticed an empty whiskey bottle near her feet and kicked it. There were several more empty bottles on the dock.

"Ralph, how come this dock is so fishy? Have you been cleaning fish here?"

"Just yesterday," Ralph answered. Sure enough, Eliza noticed the blood and guts on the pilings next to her. She laughed to think this was the place she had chosen to sit.

"There's a striped bass," Ralph said. A minute later, a large fish jumped out of the water below.

This man's instincts astonish me, Eliza thought. It's as if he can see what no one else can see.

Ralph cheerfully told her about his life, about the scar on his cheek and the scar over one eye, which he said he'd got during fights he'd had with bandits in California when he went out west for the Klondike gold rush. He related stories of his childhood, growing up on City Island with his Siwanoy Indian father, the last member of the great Turtle Clan, who buried his parents when he was still a child. Out of loneliness Ralph's father had joined the white men and had become a shipbuilder. Ralph's mother had been the daughter of a poor farmer. When Ralph's parents died of the ague, Ralph moved to Hunter Island, where he slept in the shelter of a self-built lean-to and hunted and roasted animals on spits. Sometimes Peter joined Ralph, and the two would go right from the woods to the schoolhouse, where the teachers would reprimand them for smelling like bonfires.

Eliza was mesmerized, listening to one story after another, watching Ralph's animated face, admiring his magnificent long, straight nose in profile. This man was quite a storyteller, and seemed to greatly enjoy hearing himself talk. To her relief, he didn't seem to be moving closer to her. He wasn't trying to put his arm around her or kiss her. She almost wished he would, she realized. But then what sort of trouble would she find herself in, high up on these docks?

After a while, Ralph stopped talking. He took the ends of Eliza's scarf into his hands for a minute, then moved a little closer to her. The scarf fell away from Eliza's head, leaving her hair hanging down loosely. Ralph gathered her hair in his hands, then let it fall away from his fingers.

Ralph leaned toward Eliza, and she toward him. It seemed as if he was about to kiss her but then changed his mind. She thought she smelled giant eel in his mustache, or was it stale beer or whiskey? She closed her eyes and imagined he was a Siwanoy warrior, painted for battle, paddling in a canoe up the nearby Hutchinson River.

The sun had begun to set now; the sky was turning from a light blue to cobalt blue. The wind changed and the water formed into short, rough breakers that forcefully struck the beach, one after another in fast succession. Eliza and Ralph continued to sit side by side, leaning against the damp pilings, Eliza listening to the slow, steady rhythm of Ralph's breath, which was almost in time with her own. Somewhere a cormorant screeched and seagulls cried out. Eliza hugged her knees and felt herself trembling a bit. She wondered what it might be like to touch and be touched by this man. She gave him a furtive glance; he seemed completely content to be there with her, staring out at the water. At last Eliza rose to her feet.

"It's dinnertime. I must return home before I'm missed," she said.

"I'll help you down off the docks," he replied.

In the early-evening light, with the hem of her skirts soiled, Eliza made her way across the docks, down the plank and over the beach, through the junkyard, woods, and field, back to Main Street, and finally to her own room at the parsonage.

Chapter 16

April 1904

"You look tired and anxious. You're hardly ever meeting me after school anymore. I'd like to know the reason," Sophie said pointedly. Her lips puckered in serious thought, she leaned forward and looked into Eliza's eyes as if to check her expression. Eliza swallowed as she stared out at the two stained-glass panels of ships that framed the windows in Sophie's parlor.

"I just need time to myself."

"Don't you enjoy spending time with me and Jenny anymore?"

"Yes, of course. I've just been busy," Eliza answered evasively.

"I don't even think you've been painting very much. It's Charles, isn't it? Is he pressuring you to marry him?"

"Yes. No. No more than usual. There isn't a problem with Charles." Eliza squirmed in her chair and avoided Sophie's glance. She knew Sophie had planned this conversation, and had waited until her aunt had gone to her room and Jenny had been put to bed.

Now, as usual these days, Eliza's mind wandered to thoughts of Ralph and herself: hiking with him through the distant woods beyond the bridge; building bonfires; catching fish; exploring the nearby islands in his sailboat; walking along the narrow beaches of the Sound; chasing the rats that fed at the water's edge; and then returning by herself to the parsonage, her hair in tangles, her dress soiled, and her shoes muddied.

"Eliza! Look at me, please. Talk to me."

"Yes?"

"Is everything all right at school? Are you getting along with Master Crowe?"

"I'm not sure. I think so."

"With the principal? You're standing on solid ground with him?"

"Yes."

"You're able to complete all your schoolwork, in addition to the teaching?"

"Yes," she said again.

"Eliza, are you sure you don't want to talk about Charles? How often are you seeing him?"

"Only Sunday afternoons, after church." Eliza hugged her knees and curled up in the corner of the old flowered armchair. Her short leather boots were already off, lying on the faded floral-patterned carpet. She hadn't given Charles much thought in the past month. She dared not mention Ralph, not even to Sophie.

"Did Charles try to kiss you?"

"Yes, he tried once."

"I thought so. What did you do?"

"Nothing. Believe me, it was uneventful." Eliza sighed.

140

She twisted a strand of hair around her finger and thought for a moment of Charles's slightly greasy skin and curls. Then she thought of Ralph's lithe body and the carefree way in which he tossed back his head of shiny black hair. They had not even kissed each other yet! she suddenly thought ruefully.

Sophie was firm. "Trust me when I say I don't like to interfere with your private life. However, you look tired to me. You seem agitated."

"I know," Eliza said. She wished she could tell Sophie the truth. Eventually, she knew, she would find the courage.

"Remember, you don't have to do anything you don't want to do. You can take as much time as you need to think about marriage. You're still quite young to be married. Is there anything else you would like to tell me?"

Eliza bit her lip and studied the curved yellow and green patterns on the carpeting. She scratched a mosquito bite on her calf, one of many that she'd gotten being outdoors with Ralph. On her other leg, she had a long, thin scratch from brushing her way through the briers in the woods. Her life had never been so exciting, she said to herself, yet here she was, having to hide it from her very best friend in the world! Just at that moment, Eliza heard a *pitter-pat* on the stairs and Jenny appeared in her nightdress.

"Jenny, what are you doing out of bed?" Sophie asked sternly.

"I couldn't sleep. I could hear you talking. I need a glass of water."

Sophie ran her hand along the glossy grand piano and

accompanied Jenny to the kitchen. In a few minutes, they returned with the water, which Jenny did not appear to be drinking.

"Mommy, I want to draw more pictures with Eliza."

"It's late, honey."

"Are we going to go for ice cream at Horton's Store?"

"Tomorrow's Friday. We'll go Saturday."

"Is Eliza coming with us?"

"Yes, probably. Time for bed, bunny."

Jenny grinned at Eliza mischievously. "Have you been kissing Charles?" She puckered her lips in an exaggerated fashion and made kissing sounds.

Eliza shrank down in her chair. "You listen to your mother. It's time for bed," she said.

"Are you in love with Charles?" Jenny asked.

No, Eliza thought. "Nosy, aren't you, Jen?"

"That's enough, Jenny. Go to sleep," Sophie said.

"Mommy, were you in love with Peter?"

"Yes."

"You used to kiss him, didn't you? I saw you one time."

"Jenny," Sophie warned, "no more questions now. I'm going to be angry in a minute, if you don't march up those stairs."

"If you had married Peter, we would have the same surname as Eliza, wouldn't we? Our name would be Brown instead of Long. Is that right?"

"Yes, bunny, but you're really trying my patience tonight. I'm going to count to ten. Start moving! One, two—"

142

"Mommy, I'm afraid of the dark. Will you light some more lanterns?"

"Three, four . . . move, young lady."

Jenny ran to Eliza and gave her an exuberant hug good night. The hug, so freely given, lifted Eliza's spirits. She loved this little fidget, and her mother, as she had loved Peter. Still, she felt miserable and deceitful because she was not being honest with her friend.

"I'll put her to bed," Eliza said, and escorted Jenny up the stairs.

Later, as Eliza was leaving, Sophie gave her a long, warm embrace. "When you're ready to talk to me, I'm here," she said. "I love you."

Eliza let a week go by before she met Ralph again. She waited until a lazy Saturday evening when Amanda Jane and the pastor had retired to their room early. Anytime now, Amanda Jane would be giving birth; she was irritable and anxious these days. The pastor, too, seemed preoccupied with his future role as a father. Eliza left a note on the kitchen table saying she was going out for a walk.

The night was warm, the air fresh, and the half-moon loomed large over the calm water. She hiked down Main Street and across the abandoned shipyard. There she found Ralph in his hammock. She watched for a while before waking him up.

"Sweetheart," Ralph said, "how do you do?"

Eliza laughed. Ralph was always saying that.

Ralph pulled Eliza into the hammock, and for a minute they pressed close to each other, side by side. He took her hand, then touched her arm. He kissed her on the forehead, then the mouth. Eliza kissed him back. They put their arms around each other and kissed again, longer this time. Eliza looked into Ralph's clear, dark eyes, her heart racing.

"No more," she said, sitting up. Then she got out of the hammock.

"All right," Ralph replied nonchalantly.

Ralph is as carefree as usual, Eliza thought angrily. Couldn't they have a serious conversation? Didn't he think about the future at all?

"What's the matter?" Ralph asked.

Eliza didn't answer. She was silent, and on the verge of crying.

"We shouldn't see each other anymore," she said finally.

Ralph made no reply to this at all, and Eliza filled in the silence. "I'm tired. I'm behind in my schoolwork. Master Crowe seems cross when I give in my assignments. Nothing seems to be going well."

"Sit beside me."

She sat beside him in the hammock and they put their arms around each other. It felt good.

"Is it true you are not working?" she asked.

"The winter months are far off. For now, I can live off the land," Ralph answered evasively.

"There are no jobs for you in any of the shipyards?"

"I'm waiting for a letter from my friend out West. I may work in the gold mines again."

"You're leaving?" she said, dismayed.

"I'll come back a rich man, you'll see," he answered confidently.

So he can marry me? she wondered. But that's not what he'd said. She noticed he was never specific.

"Ralph, is there any chance of a future with you?"

"There's nothing to fret over. Everything will be fine," he answered.

Eliza allowed the tears to come. "I don't know what to do! School will be over in a few months' time. I don't know if my sister will want me to live with her once the baby comes, and yet I don't want to go home to the lighthouse either. I don't have a home anymore." What she wanted to say was, I want to spend my life with you, Ralph, and I don't see how it's possible.

She wished he would tell her exactly when he was going away and when he was planning to return. Mostly she wished he would stay on the Island and find a proper profession. Maybe then he could court her publicly, in the usual way. But even then, what would her family think? she wondered. They'd try to put a stop to it.

"I like you very much, Ralph. I think I'm falling in love with you," she said.

"Me too," he answered vaguely. "I'm falling in love with you, too."

In the fold of the hammock, they moved closer together. Eliza breathed deeply, then kissed Ralph's long straight nose and imagined that he would get a job and become presentable to her family. Nearby she heard a flurry of wings as an owl took flight.

"Did you see that?" she asked.

"I've seen that owl before. I think she lives over on Hart Island and flies across sometimes."

He knows all the animals. He's magical, she thought.

They sat together in the stillness for a very long time; then Ralph ran his hand down Eliza's long hair and gathered it into a thick ponytail and let it fall. He moved in closer to her again and gently ran his hand across her back. The intimacy frightened Eliza, and she realized she needed to get up from the hammock.

"I want to go somewhere, Ralph. Right now. I want you to show me someplace beautiful."

"There is a place not far from here where a large flock of swans comes."

"That's where I want to go."

"All right," Ralph replied.

They dragged one of the canoes across the rocks and barnacles and slime and paddled out to Ralph's sailboat. Eliza unfurled the mainsail while Ralph set up the jib.

He sailed her to a place, past Hunter Island, where there was a great rolling lawn overlooking the water. He docked the boat and waited there as Eliza climbed up on the rocks and onto the lawn, where she had the sudden urge to run and jump. She stopped to pick a feather off the ground, and noticed there were others. Even in the moonlight, she could tell they were swan feathers. She felt joyful as she gathered up the feathers and put them into the pocket of her skirt. Some were small, fluffy, and the purest white; others were long and stiff and striped with brown.

"I thought you would like this place," Ralph said when Eliza had rejoined him in the boat.

"Thank you," she said.

By the time Eliza had trekked back to the parsonage, she was too exhausted to go another step. She knew it must be late; perhaps the pastor and her sister had already retired for bed. Then she noticed that all the lamps in the house were lit. Amanda Jane screamed out once, then another time, and Eliza knew that her sister's time for giving birth had come.

Chapter 17

May 1904

The new baby had fat cheeks and blue, blue eyes. He was big. Round. Enormous even. His ears were particularly large and his skin was soft and white. Eliza looked at him in wonderment: a new little person born to the world. It was an amazing thing. His hands were tiny and well formed, and his head was perfectly shaped, though too big in proportion to the rest of him—like all babies, she supposed. They'd named him Peter. Peter Lawrence. But he's nothing like the other Peter, Eliza thought as she held the heavy baby in her arms. With that round, bald head, he looks exactly like the pastor!

"Here, let me take him," Amanda Jane said, and Eliza passed her the baby as Mama looked on admiringly. Eliza hadn't realized how much she'd missed her mother. She disliked her at times, but today all she felt was love for her. Isn't life a mystery that way? she mused. Even Papa was there. Papa, who rarely stepped on dry land, now sang the sea chanteys Eliza hadn't heard him sing in years.

"We miss you at the lighthouse, daughter. Anytime you want to come home and assume your old position, you're welcome," Papa said.

Eliza stroked the baby's head and discovered that though he looked bald, little Peter had a whorl of fine, soft blond hair.

The pastor lovingly inscribed the baby's name in the family Bible. The Bible was a bulky vellum tome that had been passed down in the pastor's family for generations and had come over with his mother from England. Eliza remembered when Pastor Lawrence and Amanda Jane had written their own names in the book on their wedding day, making the vow to each other that neither would ever in their lives take a drink of alcohol.

After a time, Amanda Jane took the baby to her room for a nap. Papa returned to the lighthouse and exchanged places with Sam, who appeared at the pastor's door about two hours later. Eliza impulsively threw her arms around her brother and felt him flinch.

"What's the matter? Something seems different with you. Tell me what it is," Sam said to her.

"Nothing."

"You lie," Sam said.

"If something's different, it's that there's a new birth in the house."

Eliza studied the hard lines in her brother's brow. She felt so happy today; whatever Sam's mood, she would not let him affect her. Why God would spare a raging and drunken fool like you while taking Peter to Himself, I will never know, she thought. Just then, she turned sharply as she heard screams on the street. Leaving Sam in the parsonage, Eliza ran out the door to see what the commotion was about.

A crowd was forming on Main Street. Lord be with us! Eliza thought. There, coming down the road, rumbling and smoking, was a motorcar—the first one she had ever seen. It was also, she felt certain, the first automobile ever to come onto City Island.

The big black box shook and rattled as it made its way down the dusty road. From a distance, she could see that the driver was a young man, wearing a cap and green goggles. The driver waved to her and pulled the motorcar, gurgling and puffing, up to the side of the parsonage. It was Charles.

"Why am I not surprised it's you and still I'm surprised!" she said.

"Hop in, madam. I'm taking you for a ride," Charles said with a smug grin as he removed his goggles. He's his usual self, acting grand but looking stiff, Eliza thought.

Eliza wavered. The machine rumbled and made so much noise that she dared not approach it.

"It's a monster with glass and steel and moving parts!" she said.

"There's no danger," Charles said. He handed Eliza a long white veil, which he said would keep the dust away from her face.

"Your side doesn't have a door," Eliza stated.

"You're right. It doesn't," he said cheerfully. "I get in on the left, on your side."

Eliza slipped into the machine and held tightly on to her seat as the motorcar shook. It seemed to have a pulse like a heartbeat, but much, much louder. "Do you know how to drive this vehicle?" she asked cautiously.

"Yes! I've driven it forward and backward. I've driven in circles and figure eights. It's wonderful, as you'll soon see for yourself!" Charles said excitedly.

"All right, then. I trust you!" Eliza said.

"Here, I'll show you how it works," Charles said authoritatively. He put the goggles back down over his eyes with a determined expression. "First we push out the clutch, then we move the gear level into low speed. This has to be done very carefully. Then we release the clutch and I put my foot down on this pedal. Hold on, Eliza! We're off!"

With a sudden jerk, the motorcar bounded away, turned, and headed up Main Street. Eliza felt her stomach tighten and her eyes widen, but soon she found the ride so thrilling, so absolutely terrific, she forgot her fears. The automobile was going fast, ten miles an hour or so, much faster than she could ride Amanda Jane's bicycle. Everywhere, people ran out of their houses waving. She knew the whole Island was watching her. Carriages pulled out of the way. A large yellow dog chased after the motorcar until it could no longer keep pace with it.

"The Devil's machine!" an old woman called from her open window.

Charles drove across City Island Bridge, through the wooded parklands, then across a second bridge to the town of Pelham. They drove by woods, and grand houses, and a railroad station. They passed a stable and a dairy farm. "Here we go—a hill!" Charles said. Up the motorcar went, then down again, gaining speed. They were now racing along a road that followed the curving shoreline, with a view of the Pelham woods across the water. Eliza begged him to turn around, but he simply grinned. She closed her eyes in terror. A few minutes later, she opened her eyes, and was filled with delight at the sight before her.

"Look, Charles, look!" Eliza said. For there, surrounded by waves and rocks and small passenger boats and two large schooners, was her lighthouse, a brick doll-sized building in the middle of the Sound. How tiny it seemed! The seas were busy today, full of small motorized dories, a Hell's Gate pilot boat, two cargo schooners, and a steamboat. Most of the vessels followed what was more or less a straight-line shipping route past the lighthouse. From this vantage point, the reef to the far side of the lighthouse did indeed look like stepping-stones. This was a view belonging only to birds, Eliza thought; it was as if she were flying.

City Island formed a long thin strip, she realized as the tower of Trinity Church and the roof of the parsonage emerged from the treetops. Eliza saw very clearly now the route she had rowed across the water to and from school for so many years. She saw the terrace of the lighthouse where she used to fish and catch crabs and eels and skip rope. What surprised her the most was not how different everything looked from this perspective, but how easily she recognized it all. The landscape hadn't changed, exactly; all that she knew was there, but now as part of a much larger panorama.

"That was a marvelous ride," Eliza told Charles at the end of the day.

"Would you care to have dinner with me this evening?"

"No, I'm afraid not," she said, thinking she'd try to sneak out of the house to meet Ralph.

"I almost never see you anymore. I get the feeling you're not in love with me."

"Oh, Charles," she said. "No, I'm not in love with you, but you've just given me the best day of my entire life."

Chapter 18

May 1904, later the same day

After dinner at the parsonage, Eliza looked for Ralph in all his usual spots: the abandoned shipyard, Hunter Island, and along the beaches of the Pelham shoreline. She hadn't seen him for a week or more, and was now beginning to grow a little frantic. If he was indeed in town, she thought it odd that she hadn't chanced upon him on Main Street. Ralph, like most of the men on the Island, liked to sit on the storefront stoops and exchange gossip with the villagers. Surely he had not left for the gold mines in California without saying good-bye?

The Bucket of Blood. Oh! There's where he would likely be on a Saturday evening, Eliza realized. So, on Amanda Jane's fancy three-wheeled bicycle, she pedaled up and down Main Street around the vicinity of the saloon in the hope of meeting him. Finally she parked the bicycle around the side of the saloon, and was on the point of daring to enter the building when she spotted

Alfred, arm in arm with Carlotta Proudfit, taking a stroll in the cool spring air.

"Eliza, what a nice surprise to see you," Alfred called out cheerfully. "I hear you're doing wonderfully well in your teaching position."

"It's going quite well, I believe."

"Congratulations! Aren't you bully? I must say, though, Master Crowe's class is by far the duller and quieter without you."

"Yes, it is," added Carlotta, who was clad today in a tailor-made spring suit—a white shirtwaist with a gingham string necktie and an ankle-length skirt—and high-laced boots.

"How is your Mr. Boxley?" Alfred asked pointedly.

"Enjoying all the inventions of our modern age. He's gotten himself a motorcar."

"So he's the one with the car? I might have guessed! I got a glimpse of it today, roaring down Main Street. Isn't that just the thing?"

As Alfred took Carlotta's white-gloved hand, Eliza said her good-bye and darted away from the couple as quickly as she could. She waited at the wharf behind the saloon until they were out of sight. It would have been Eliza herself walking with Alfred, if things had worked out differently and if she'd taken a fancy to him. She couldn't blame Alfred for having another lady friend, she mused. And meanwhile, there was Ralph to consider.

Once more, Eliza approached the Bucket of Blood. She cautiously opened the saloon's heavy door and slipped inside the darkened room. There rough-looking sailors crouched over the bar, mugs in hand. Talk and laughter filled the crowded, smoky room, along with loud ragtime music. As far as Eliza could tell, Ralph was not among these men. Against the far wall, a man played a well-worn upright piano, and around the piano stood several women in garish red dresses laced up tightly at the waist and left full and open at the top. Eliza eyed them with fascination. They were painted ladies, who, no doubt, traveled back and forth from the back door of the saloon to the ships docked in the adjacent boatyard. Eliza stood there frozen, not knowing what to do.

Behind the bar, a heavy, leering man with a curled, waxed mustache beckoned to Eliza. "What will you have to drink, miss?"

"Nothing, sir. Not right now, sir."

One of the painted ladies, a large blond woman, swaggered over to Eliza and stood behind her at the bar. "What can I do for you?" she asked. "Are you looking for someone?"

"Ralph. Is he here tonight?"

"Oh, I see, he's taken himself a pretty young miss, has he? That's Ralph! Well, my dear, pull up a stool and let old May buy you a drink." She motioned to the man with the curled mustache as she seated herself on one of the barstools. "Tom, give us two mugs of beer. It isn't often we get the company of young ladies from the outside."

Eliza took her seat and tried not to stare at May's plump, middle-aged body, revealed through her scant red dress. The very idea of talking to a painted lady horrified her, and yet she found she did not dislike May. She soon felt herself starting to like her.

156

"What's your name, love? Speak out loud over the music."

"Eliza Brown."

"I'm May," the lady said, offering her hand. "Pleased to meet you."

"Do you know Ralph?" Eliza put in.

"Everyone knows Ralph, love."

"I'm afraid Ralph's gone west to mine for gold. He left without even saying good-bye to me!"

Eliza stared at the foaming mug, then took a tiny sip. The beer tasted a little bitter, though it wasn't intolerable. She forced herself to take a larger gulp, then added, "Ralph said he'd go back to the gold mines in California one of these days."

May and Tom the bartender broke into a fit of laughter. Then May said kindly, "Once a man came into the saloon and told stories of the Klondike gold rush. Ralph talked to him for hours. I think that's where his story must have come from, though you never know with Ralph."

"That's right," Tom said, filling a mug of beer for himself. "Ralph won himself some gold nuggets from the man in a poker game. I think it *is* true he was in Pennsylvania one year mining coal."

"Oh, May. Ralph lied to me! He never was part of the Klondike gold rush, was he? I suppose he wasn't employed to dive for buried treasure in Florida, either." Eliza frowned, then took another gulp of her drink.

May put a white, flabby arm around Eliza. "Bless you, my dear! Ralph does tell tales. Do you care about him very much?"

157

Eliza nodded, and bit her lip. "I thought I did. Now I don't know. I've been such a fool!"

"Ralph is a charmer, he surely is, and I can't say I blame you for admiring him."

"He lied to me. I thought he cared about me."

"I'm sure he does, love."

Eliza looked morosely down at her mug, then stared at the swirling patterns of raised velvet on the wallpaper. She ran her hand along the smooth mahogany of the bar. Feeling a bit light-headed now, she picked up her mug.

Tom curled the waxed ends of his mustache with his pinkie finger. He no longer seemed scary to Eliza. "Listen, miss," he said, "you seem a very nice, decent girl. I'd be remiss if I did not tell you to stay away from Ralph! There's a woman with child who came from Pennsylvania a few days ago looking for Ralph, and says he's the father."

"That's probably why we haven't seen Ralph," May offered before taking a drink from her mug. "Poor Eliza! I'm sure Ralph's hiding someplace in the woods until it all blows over." She sighed. "That's Ralph—dodging trouble, disappearing for a few weeks or months, then reappearing."

"Ralph's been arrested for being in brawls and has been jailed several times. Still, he's a dandy fellow, Ralph is, isn't he, May?" Tom volunteered.

"Our boy's excellent company, and I'll never speak against him, Tom. But hurting our friend here is another thing. I don't like to see the child learn the cruel lessons of life this way. Wait until Ralph hears from Aunty May!"

158

"Aunty?" Eliza repeated. "Ralph's mother is your sister?"

"No, child," May said with a laugh. "I don't know of *any* folk related to Ralph. Do you, Tom?"

"The man's a mystery," Tom agreed.

Eliza suddenly felt sick to her stomach. The night was becoming nightmarish. "May, I've been such a fool," she said, slurring her words a bit. "Ralph told me he was the son of a noble Siwanoy Indian warrior and I believed him! I should have known better. There are no more Siwanoys left in Pelham, are there?"

"All killed by the white men or driven away," May said sadly.

"I don't know what to believe. Maybe it doesn't matter. I'll never see him again. I feel hot, and very peculiar, May." May's friendly round face suddenly looked blurred to Eliza, then came into focus again.

Just then Sam pushed his way through the crowd of men. "If it isn't my little sister from the parsonage, having a drink with Big May!" he bellowed.

"Sam!" Eliza uttered. Naturally, Sam seemed to know the painted ladies of the saloon.

"You're drunk, too, from the looks of it. Hello, Tom. I'll have some blackberry brandy. What are you two girls talking about? Is my bookish sister teaching you Latin, May?"

"Your sister's had her heart broken by Ralph, and Tom and me have just bought her a beer."

"Ralph! I'll kill him when I see him."

"Don't you grow hot on us, Sam," warned May. "Let's

not have any fights now. Your sweet little sister here is not used to drinking. I think you'd better escort her home."

"We're leaving, Eliza, just as soon as I finish this one drink," Sam said, gulping down the blackberry brandy.

"Thank you, May," Eliza said wanly. She could hardly hold her head up now. "You've been so kind. . . . One more question, May."

"Anything, duck."

Eliza paused, thinking she might not want to hear the answer to her question.

"What is it, love?"

"Did you know my brother Peter Brown?"

"Ah, Peter!" May said, her eyes lighting up. "He was the shy, lanky fellow who had a room in the boarding-house. Passionate about ships he was."

"May used to cut his hair sometimes," Sam said.

"Yes. It just about killed us all to hear he was drowned. He was as fine a man as ever I knew—not that he ever went off with any of us girls," she added, looking toward Eliza.

"Let me try some of that blackberry brandy," Eliza told Sam. She held the glass to her lips, and the sweet liquid burned down her throat.

"Let's go, little sister," Sam said with more compassion than he usually showed Eliza.

Eliza said good-bye to May and Tom and allowed herself to be pulled through the crowd by Sam. Outside, the cool air made her feel a bit better, though the trees looked fuzzy as she staggered up Main Street holding on to Sam's arm. The land seemed to rock, as if she were standing on her old rowboat, the one she used to take to school. "I feel so hot, Sam, so strange. I think the trees are talking to me. You seem different to me tonight too, Sam, almost as if you were kind, like our Peter. It won't last, will it? Sam, I was in love, and I've made such a fool of myself. Have you ever been in love, Sam? If you had I imagine you would not be so horrible to us all. I thought he was part Siwanoy Indian. Maybe it doesn't matter. . . . I wonder if my true love has gone back to the coal mines in Pennsylvania or whether he's hiding in the woods near here. Or perhaps he's gone to California to mine for gold—"

"Quiet, girl! We'll be home soon. Do you think you're going to be sick?"

"Sick? No, not yet," she said. "I just feel so hot."

"Eliza Brown, is that you?" a distant voice called out. Eliza was only vaguely aware of someone's calling her name, and when she turned her head, she didn't see anyone.

"Let's hurry. See if you can walk just a bit faster," Sam coaxed.

Eliza looked down at her feet, not caring that one shoe was unbuttoned. She stared at the pebbles and the crushed oyster shells in the dirt road. "There are pretty shells in the road, aren't there, Sam? Do you like the new baby? He's adorable, isn't he? Isn't it odd that May used to cut our Peter's hair? Do you know I can't remember his face anymore but I do remember the way his hair felt, the thickness of it. Just now I thought I heard a stern voice call out my name. Now I think I must have imagined it."

Sam turned as if he, too, might have heard someone

call out. "Eliza," he said, with a touch of worry in his voice. "You didn't have a coat on tonight when you went out, did you?"

"No, it was so warm I went out without my coat. . . . I think I did ride the bicycle, though. I left it around the side of the saloon, along with some other bicycles that were there. Oh, Sam, I'm hot, and my head is spinning."

"As soon as we get to the house, I'm going to go back to the saloon and get the bicycle. Eliza, I suggest you go straight to bed. I wonder if we're going to get out of this mess. Oh, little sister, I thought *I* was a fool!"

Chapter 19

"What's going on?" the pastor thundered as Eliza stumbled into the front entranceway of the parsonage.

"Eliza isn't feeling well. She's just on her way to bed," Sam said, holding Eliza by the arm.

"Wait. Eliza, I've looked all over the Island for you!" the pastor said. "You've been drinking, both of you. Sam, you have done a very bad thing by leading your sister astray."

"It wasn't Sam's fault," Eliza managed to say. She seated herself in a chair and put her hands up to her head, trying to steady herself.

"Eliza, you are not to leave this parsonage, except to go to school, and you are never again to drink alcohol," warned the pastor. "Am I understood?"

"Yes, sir," Eliza answered miserably.

Eliza looked at the little oak desk where the pastor had been writing. "You've got my journal there! How dare you!" she said coldly, as clearly as she could say the words.

She ran over to the pastor and tried to take it from him, but suddenly the parlor spun around and the candlesticks on the fireplace seemed to move apart, then together again. She sat herself down in the pastor's chair to keep from falling.

"You've betrayed our trust. I looked for you tonight and couldn't find you anywhere. If I hadn't thought you were in danger, I wouldn't have read your journal. Besides, I'd only just begun to read it."

"You are a liar and a hypocrite," Eliza slurred out, her head pounding. "I'm getting to like Sam, in fact. He's no good and he's a bully, but at least he doesn't pretend he's something he isn't!"

"You're obviously in no condition to discuss the matter now," Pastor Lawrence said, his eyes fiery.

Amanda Jane entered the room with her arms crossed. In a hoarse, angry voice, she said, "I'm warning you all. Whatever is going on, I want quiet now. I want Sam out of this house!"

"Calm yourself, dear. It's all under control," the pastor said.

"Don't worry, *I'm* not going to stay here. I prefer the company of the boardinghouse!" Sam yelled. From the pastor and Amanda Jane's bedroom, baby Peter now started to shriek. Amanda Jane ran to tend him, and a few moments later Sam left the parsonage, slamming the door behind him. Eliza then found her way to her bedroom, where she quickly collapsed into sleep.

In the morning, Eliza was tired and sick. Her neck felt stiff and her head ached. She could barely muster up enough spirit to wash and dress herself. The pastor gave

164

her a short lecture about how alcohol was a curse and an atrocity. All the saloonkeepers who sold it ought to be drummed out of society, he said. Eliza wished she could go back to bed, especially when Amanda Jane presented a list of household duties to be done.

"I won't tell Mother," she started out. "I must say, though, the pastor and I have made the mistake of being far too lax with you. Certain things will have to change in this household. Daily, not just occasionally, I need you to help me sweep the kitchen, dust, clean, fill the lamps, wash the dishes, and make the beds. And on Saturdays and Sundays, there'll be baking. Is today's ironing finished yet? Did you remember to dip the collars and shirt-fronts into starch before pressing them?"

After a week of chores, Eliza wrote in her sketchbook journal:

> *Living here with a curfew is just the same as being confined to the lighthouse. Fiddlesticks. I'll never again go back to Ralph. Yet I must admit I miss him, despite everything. I wonder where he is and how he is doing.*
>
> *A week has passed since that awful incident in the saloon. I've since confessed everything to Sophie. Though she disapproved of Ralph, she has not withdrawn her friendship from me. Thankfully Amanda Jane and the pastor never learned the whole truth. I will never forgive the pastor for reading my journal but it's lucky that he assumed I'd made up all the stories about going places in boats at night.*
>
> *There is one more worry I have. Sam was not able to*

find Amanda Jane's bicycle when he returned to the
saloon that night. Someone must have stolen it!

"Cheer up," Sophie whispered as she gave Eliza's hand a squeeze.

At the front of the church, near the altar, Pastor Lawrence sprinkled water over baby Peter's chubby face. This baby's so big, he barely fits into his little lace outfit, Eliza thought. Baby Peter opened his eyes wide, surprised that his father was pouring water on him, but he didn't cry. The pastor spoke the blessing and handed the big baby to his wife. The church was nearly full today and Eliza's whole family was there, everyone except Papa, who was keeping the Light.

The morning was hot and, not having eaten breakfast, Eliza felt a little delirious. She knew she was losing weight. Her shoulders were stiff and her back ached from the previous night's scrubbing with the washboard. Her hair spread about her in long, loose, curly tangles. Next to her, Jenny fidgeted. "Later we'll draw pictures," Eliza promised her.

The whole congregation stood and recited prayers for the baby, then sat down again. Amanda Jane took her seat in the front pew, beside Mama.

Another forty minutes to go, Eliza thought. She listened to the sermon with half an ear; it was something about brotherly love. Bored, she turned her head to watch the faces of the people in the church. There was Alfred, five rows behind her, tucked in beside Carlotta Proudfit, with her yards of dresses. The passage of time had made her think better of Alfred. He was a nice man and he was learning an honest trade. Why hadn't she taken more of a liking to him? Her previous complaints about him didn't seem important now.

Then, sure enough, there was waxy Charles Boxley in his brown suit, a few rows behind Alfred, sitting by Mrs. Boxley and looking absolutely expressionless. The minute the service was over, Charles would come over to her. She dreaded it, in a way. But then again, tea at the Boxleys' might be a pleasant diversion this afternoon, if she could persuade the pastor to allow her to go.

All at once Eliza's heart stopped. The door at the back of the church opened, and there was Ralph, strutting up the center aisle. He took a seat behind Eliza. Isn't he looking dandy today, though, Eliza said to herself, with his hair cut. He wore a freshly ironed shirt, and even a ribbon tie! He looked at Eliza for only a second and then calmly centered his attention straight ahead, as if listening to the sermon. He doesn't fool me a bit, Eliza thought. The audacity!

"Sophie, there's *Ralph*," Eliza said under her breath.

"Hush. Don't pay him any mind," Sophie answered.

Communion followed, and Eliza slowly walked up to the altar and knelt, cupping her hands to receive the Host. Ralph followed her and knelt beside her. Eliza noticed that he was out of turn, that he hadn't waited for the usher to signal that it was time for his pew. He looks so reverent here with his knees bent, Eliza thought; the Devil himself couldn't put on a finer display of false piety. Then she realized with horror that Ralph had the smell of liquor on his breath!

After receiving the wafer and the sweet grape nectar,

Eliza returned to her seat, her ears hot and her lips stiff with consternation. Pastor Lawrence continued to administer the sacrament as usual, while Ralph sat calmly in his seat.

The minute the service ended, Ralph stomped down the aisle of the church and out the front door. At the entranceway, a crowd gathered. Eliza attempted to slip out the side of the church but was stopped by Charles.

Charles wore his usual vacant half smile. He doesn't have the vaguest notion about anything on earth, Eliza thought as he whispered something in her ear. He seemed to say "I'm not annoying you on purpose," though she couldn't quite make out the words.

"You're not annoying me on purpose?" Eliza repeated out loud. Perhaps Charles Boxley was far more perceptive than she had imagined!

"Silly girl!" Charles grinned at her. "What a sense of humor you have! I said I'm not *ignoring* you on purpose."

Poor Charles! Was she hurting his feelings? But never mind about that just now, she told herself; she had to make her way out the door before Ralph accosted her in front of the congregation.

"Want to go for a ride with me in the motorcar today?"

"Charles, I need to return to the parsonage right away. I think I'm going to be ill!"

Alfred appeared next from out of the crowd. "How are you, Eliza?" he asked cheerfully. "Congratulations on the christening of your new nephew. What a fine, healthy baby!"

"Thank you," Eliza replied hurriedly. "See you another time."

Finally Eliza made her way out the side door. She dashed around the corner of the church and was only a few yards short of the parsonage when she realized Ralph had spotted her. In a wink he had caught up to her.

Ralph grabbed Eliza by the sleeve. She stopped trying to run away, and they stood together underneath the old oak tree.

"I need to talk to you," he said.

Eliza crossed her arms and studied the hard ground and the raised tree roots below her feet.

"I have a gift for you, for your birthday." Ralph handed her a necklace made of oyster shells, strung crudely together as if he had made the present himself.

"My birthday was months ago." Eliza fingered the smooth shells of the necklace, then handed it back to him. "I can't accept a gift from you. You lied to me, about everything!"

"I never lied to you."

"You lie constantly, Ralph! You have a lady friend back in Pennsylvania, don't you?"

"No. I never had a lady friend there. That was nothing, only tales people told—"

She did not let him finish his sentence. "You never were a diver off Florida and you never mined for gold in California!"

"Who says I'm not a diver? Who says I didn't mine for gold? I'm definitely going back to California to work again, just as soon as I receive a card from my friend."

Eliza looked into Ralph's dark eyes. They were a little bloodshot around the corners. But he seemed sincere. Even now, she couldn't hate him. Yet she must stay away from him, at all costs, she told herself. Already she could feel herself weakening, just a little, as Ralph moved a step closer to her and touched her hair. He tried to kiss her.

She pushed him away. "No! Go, and leave me alone. I don't ever want to see you again!" she said hotly. Then she started to cry.

He gently placed his hands on her shoulders. "Listen to me, please."

She squirmed away from him.

"Sweetheart, I went to the altar this morning and a feeling poured over me. I've had a spiritual awakening."

"There you go, telling your tales. Lie number one," she said.

"I'm going to start attending services regularly."

"Ralph, that's lie number two."

"I'm going to change my ways—"

"Lie number three!" she said. How could he stand there with alcohol on his breath talking about how he was going to change his ways!

"I caught three large bluefish. Want me to bring them to your house?"

"No!" she answered, and stamped her foot. "Go away and don't come back here again. Ever."

Just at that point Sam ran over, wearing his Sunday

best. His face looked red and stern. "It's Ralph back again, is it?" he said.

After some more words were exchanged, Sam punched Ralph in the chest and the two became enmeshed in violent hitting and kicking. Sam hit Ralph on the nose and Ralph staggered backward. After he'd regained his balance, he gritted his teeth and ran at Sam, aiming for his throat and eyes. Ralph's nose was bloody and he had an intense, hateful look in his eyes as he pushed Sam away with his boot. Eliza feared for her brother's life. This man was a real fighter, she saw. Ralph kicked Sam in the chest and Sam fell to the ground on top of the big roots of the tree. Ralph was just about to kick Sam in the head when Eliza forced herself in between the men.

"Don't you kill him, Ralph!" she yelled.

"Hey, hey," the pastor said, entering the scene and attempting to help a few others hold Ralph back from Sam. "Stop this now or I'll fetch the police."

A crowd of parishioners, on their way to the christening party at the parsonage, formed a circle around the fighters. Master Crowe was among them, as well as Hosiah Prim, Charles Boxley, and Alfred. Amanda Jane held baby Peter tightly, and Mama clutched Amanda Jane's arm. I couldn't be a bigger spectacle than I am right now, Eliza thought with shame.

Eliza helped Sam to his feet while the pastor kept Ralph at arm's distance. "I'm warning you to stay away from my sister," said Sam after he'd caught his breath. "Find yourself a lady friend from the Bucket of Blood, why don't you? Everyone knows you're trash, Ralph, and you don't belong around the likes of my family! If you ever try to touch Eliza again, I swear you'll be a dead man."

Mama stepped forward and pulled Eliza back. "Eliza! Amanda Jane and everyone. Go into the house."

Chapter 20

May 1904, the next morning

Eliza walked about the schoolroom and closed the windows to keep out the gusts of spring rain. Outside, in the twiggy ends of the wet branches of the maple tree, two round, plump sparrows hopped about, chirping. Inside, along the windowsill, seedling sunflower plants grew in glass petri dishes, one for each of the class's five girls and sixteen boys. Eliza tried to appear cheerful, despite her worries. She proudly looked around the room at the children and the way they were sitting quietly in their seats. That was no small achievement for this class.

"Class, please turn to your McGuffey readers, page forty-nine. Lizzie, you have a dramatic flair for reading out loud. Why don't you begin?"

Lizzie opened her *Eclectic Reader* and read an excerpt from Washington Irving's "The Wife."

A stocky, square-bodied boy interrupted. "Miss Brown, I thought you were going to read from *The Iliad* today. I don't like this dumb old essay."

Another boy snickered. "I don't want to hear about 'the softer sex,' either!"

Eliza shook her head and frowned.

"Leave Miss Brown alone," Justin piped up. "Can't you see she's upset?"

"Thank you, Justin. Class, let me just say this one thing: It's more important than ever that you all behave," Eliza said with a deep sigh. Her eye caught a glimpse of the children's "time-line" mural, which wrapped around the room and showed all the major events of the world in pictures. All of life seemed to be crumbling around her, yet she still enjoyed seeing her pupils' handiwork. She would become a good teacher after all.

Justin and two other boys read out loud; then Eliza wrote the next day's homework assignment on the blackboard. "You shall be responsible for knowing how to spell and define the following words from the lesson," she said, and wrote, "1. fortitude 2. overwhelming 3. disaster—"

Eliza put down the chalk when she noticed Hosiah Prim through the windowpane of the classroom door. The short, bright-eyed principal quietly entered. "Please meet me in my office today at four-thirty," he said brusquely.

"Yes, sir," Eliza answered before Mr. Prim slipped away. For goodness' sake, what now? she thought. She felt the muscles of her face tighten as she gazed out the window. The sparrows were still there, chirping joyfully. Eliza finished writing the vocabulary words on the board and said, "Let's continue our lesson. Does anyone know the meaning of *fortitude*?"

The day dragged by. There was only one day in her memory that was more terrible, which was the day she had waited in the parsonage for Peter's body to be brought home. What she wouldn't do to talk to Peter again, if only for a few minutes, she said to herself. At least it was a comfort to know that Sophie was nearby. Kind, sweet Sophie.

At four-thirty, Eliza walked down the long first-floor corridor, past the assembly room and library to Mr. Prim's office. When she entered, she caught her breath, surprised to see Master Crowe there as well, sitting stiff and upright on the principal's plush red sofa.

"Take a seat, Eliza," said Mr. Prim, offering her a chair across from his desk. Master Crowe greeted her with a nod.

Eliza waited, her knees trembling underneath her purple organdy dress.

"Firstly, I want to say you've done a fine job in taming the rougher youths of your class. I see you are also very popular with the children. However . . ." The principal paused and tapped his pen on his desk blotter.

"Yes?" Eliza asked expectantly.

"However, it has been brought to my attention that your conduct has been far from demure. You have behaved in a manner utterly unfitting for a scholar, let alone a teacher, of City Island School." The principal unfolded a piece of notebook paper covered with Master Crowe's graceful, curving penmanship and continued. "Point one. I have noted that on Thursday, September seventeen, 1903, you were handed back a composition in which you stated, 'Christ was a married man.' "

"I said he *might* have been married," Eliza retorted angrily. "I have no idea what the truth is about that."

"On the same day, I have noted, you uttered the blasphemous statement, 'Christ was married to Mary Magdalene.' Point two."

"This was nearly a year ago, and I don't see why you're bringing the subject up now," Eliza answered, looking toward the balding, clean-shaven Master Crowe. The teacher appeared triumphant, though the wart on the end of his nose still resembled a drip.

"Mr. Crowe has said that on numerous occasions he has caught you drawing in class—point three—including Tuesday, November ten—point four—in which he confiscated a scandalous caricature you'd made of him."

Eliza gave the principal a pleading look, then turned toward Master Crowe. "I'm sorry. I didn't mean anything by it. I just like to draw."

"Were you or were you not forbidden to draw in class?"

"You did tell me, sir."

"Were you or were you not generously given by this school a chance to be a teacher? Have you or have you not disgraced yourself repeatedly?" said Master Crowe. "Please continue, Mr. Prim."

"Furthermore, we have record of several latenesses in the fall—point five. Point six, you have not attended your senior classes with any regularity."

"How can I attend the senior classes if I am teaching the fourth grade? I've not missed a single day teaching."

"Point seven. Thursday, December seventeen, you lost control of the fourth-grade scholars and Master Crowe caught two of the boys running through the hallway. Then, point eight, on Friday, March nineteen, at twelve-thirty P.M., Mr. Crowe overheard a certain conversation with Mrs. Sophie Long in which you were standing near the ladies' lavatory on the second floor. At that time, you made reference to having stolen twenty-one petri dishes from the upper-grade science room."

Enraged, Eliza stood up, put her hands on Mr. Prim's desk, and leaned toward him. "Sir, I did not steal the petri dishes. I borrowed them. There are three more dusty boxes of spare petri dishes in the supply cabinet on the third floor. This is sounding like an inquisition, sir."

"Please sit down, Miss Brown. Thank you. I have but two points left to review. These are quite serious indeed. I have listed here that Mr. Crowe was walking his sheepdog on Saturday, April seventeen, at ten-thirty P.M. and that he saw you at that time, in a drunken stupor, exit the Paradise Saloon with a young man. This incident has been confirmed by the fact that Mr. Crowe found your bicycle outside of this disreputable establishment."

"He had no right to take the bicycle. It is my sister's bicycle."

"The bicycle will be returned to you after this meeting. It is parked right outside the window of this office and you are welcome to retrieve it at a later point. Were you or were you not intoxicated by alcohol on the evening of April seventeen?"

"I regret to say I was, sir."

"I see," the principal answered gruffly, and twitched his mustache. Mr. Crowe cleared his throat.

"Finally, point ten. I understand there was a fight yesterday, Sunday, April twenty-five, between your brother and a certain undesirable named Ralph. Reference was made to your carrying on a liaison with this man Ralph."

At the mention of Ralph, Eliza felt her heart stop, then start again. She looked from one pale face to the other and said nothing.

"Seeing there are so many points of contention that go against our *Rules for Teachers,* Eliza," the principal continued, "I am expelling you from City Island School. You are not to set foot in this school again, as either teacher or scholar. Am I understood?"

"Yes," Eliza muttered, sinking back in her chair. I want to die, she thought. I would be happier dead; I wish they would kill me now.

"Wait, Mr. Prim," she said, mustering up some courage. "Please let me talk to you alone."

Master Crowe reluctantly left the room, closing the door behind him.

"Yes, miss?"

"I'm guilty of much of what you say, yet this ugly list doesn't describe me at all. City Island School has been a big part of my life for many years. I've loved attending this school. Hasn't my record so far been flawless? Haven't I received the highest marks?"

"No one would argue that," answered Mr. Prim. "Also, you did a fine job with the Christmas pageant. Mr. Crowe only brought forth the allegations because, as your teacher and supervisor, it is his duty to help you in every way possible to be an upright citizen. Your separation from the school was designed to help you bring forth your best—"

"Then, please, sir. Won't you consider giving me the

opportunity to earn my diploma? It's just under eight weeks till graduation, Mr. Prim. If I don't have the diploma, I'll *never* be able to be a teacher."

Mr. Prim thoughtfully stroked his goatee, and tapped his pen on the desk a few more times. Then he folded Master Crowe's paper. "I'm afraid you'll never teach now anyway, miss," he said, and paused. "I will say this to you: Seeing that you've had a strong record, I will tell Master Crowe that you may continue your assignments independently. When you have successfully completed your work, you may receive your diploma, despite the fact that you will not be graduating with your class."

"Thank you. I'm grateful to you, sir."

Eliza trudged back to the parsonage, guiding Amanda Jane's three-wheeled bicycle beside her. The air was much cooler now; the rain had stopped. There were daffodils outside the schoolhouse as well as in some of the villagers' gardens, along with purple crocuses. The lawns were green. There was green everywhere, though the trees were still mostly without their leaves. Outside the parsonage, near the principal's office, a cherry tree bloomed. Peter, I wish you had lived to see the springtime, she said silently.

Inside the parsonage, Amanda Jane rocked baby Peter. The house smelled of roasted chicken, the pastor's favorite dish. "I've just fed and burped the baby. Soon he'll be ready to sleep," Amanda Jane said, and Eliza told her she would like a turn in holding him. Amanda Jane passed the bundle of baby and blankets to her sister.

Peter looked up at Eliza with his clear, round blue eyes as if transfixed for a moment, and then he smiled. He now recognized her, she was sure. Eliza held the warm, powder-smelling bundle to her. She marveled at Peter's tiny, perfect hands and tiny stockinged feet, which kept moving in circles. This baby boy, so big and rosy and healthy, will be sure to outlive us all, Eliza thought with satisfaction.

Eliza waited for a long time before she brought up the subject of her dismissal. "Amanda Jane, something horrible has happened. I wanted to tell you first, especially since you have been so kind as to take me into your home."

"Oh? Tell me what the trouble is."

Eliza told her the story, and Amanda Jane sat bewildered, looking a little paler each moment. "Eliza, the baby's asleep now. I'll take him and put him in the cradle," she said. "Talk to Lawrence. He's in his study, writing the sermon for the week. We'll have supper after your meeting." Then, once more, Eliza prepared herself to relate the dreaded news.

Pastor Lawrence stopped writing and rested his fountain pen on a china pen tray when Eliza entered the room. He pushed aside the high stacks of books and papers on his small maple desk, giving Eliza his full attention.

"I'll be ready to leave the house in the morning," Eliza ended by saying.

"This is your home now, Eliza, and I hope you will stay."

"I thought you'd send me back to the lighthouse. It's a disgrace to have me living here in the parsonage. What will the parishioners think?" she said.

"You've suffered so much," he answered with a sigh.

"Don't let the neighbors' opinions concern you. I suppose it will be good for them to have to grow a little—likewise myself. Perhaps I've paid too much attention to my work and the new baby. Forgive me if I've neglected you, Eliza! Please forgive me, as well, for looking at your journal, which I should not have done without your permission. Now, we shall pray together. *Father, we thank you for Eliza—may she find peace within herself; for Mr. Crowe and Mr. Prim, for Amanda Jane and baby Peter and my own life; and we pray for Mr. Ralph. Amen.*"

"You prayed for Ralph," Eliza said, stunned. She felt something in her heart break loose, and she started to cry. Many times the pastor had surprised her for the worse; this time he had surprised her for the better. An image came to her mind of all the people in the congregation, the poorest workers from the shipyard as well as the well-to-do ladies of the church. Her brother-in-law had welcomed them all. Eliza suddenly felt very proud to know the pastor. Despite his stiffness and formality and his terrible misdeed of having looked at her journal, he was actually a very fine human being.

"Dear girl," the pastor said with weariness in his voice. "As a minister of God, sometimes I am on the mark and sometimes perhaps not. I wonder if I'm able to address my congregation's true concerns. I have learned one thing in my years, however: If the prayer doesn't include everyone, the prayer isn't right."

In the cool of the early morning, even before the sound of baby Peter's first cry, Eliza put on her old gray cotton work dress. She packed her new organdy frock and her

181

other clothes, her sketchbook, and her two photographs of Peter. Then she left a note on her pillow. Briefly she said good-bye to the cherry tree outside her window and the flowers and vegetables she had planted in the garden. She hoped the sunflowers would come up. The pastor's rowboat was just where she had left it last, tied to a post on the beach. High tide was fast approaching, she was glad to see, so she wouldn't have to drag the boat far.

The crosscurrents made rowing a difficult task that morning, but the exercise helped her clear her mind. The winds picked up force; perhaps there would be a storm later in the day, she thought. On the shore, she saw from a distance, the bare trees were whipping back and forth. The trip to the Stepping Stones took her almost a full hour.

Papa was waiting on the lighthouse landing dock when she approached. He must have spotted her with his spyglass.

How rare to have a moment when just the two of them were together, Eliza thought. She knew that from Papa there would be no questions about why she was there, and probably no reprimands once he learned why.

"Eliza," he said. "I am very glad to see you, though I wish you would not brave the waters alone. Was there no one to accompany you today?"

"I've told you many times, I'm old enough to take a boat out alone."

"Yes. I see now that you are. From now on you shall row yourself. So be it. Welcome, daughter."

"Papa," she said. "I've come home to stay."

Chapter 21

June 1904

"Long ago, before this lighthouse was built, the Devil visited this place, Jenny," Eliza began, "when the forests of Connecticut and New York were rich and green and peopled by the Siwanoy Indians. The evil one, called Habbomoko, tried to claim the best land for himself, but the Siwanoy braves chased him with slings and arrows out of their village and down the coast. When Habbomoko reached this place, where the Devil's Belt is at its narrowest point, he created rocks so that he could use them as stepping-stones, to cross to the opposite shore. Everywhere Habbomoko stepped, a new boulder appeared. Then, once on the opposite shore, he hurled as many boulders as he could at the Indians, which explains why one side of the coast is rocky and the other is smooth. Or some say it's because of something called a glacier."

"What happened to the Devil?" Jenny asked.

"Still lurking around, to be sure. See those rocks there, Jen? Every one of them is part of a treacherous underwater reef that can rip the bottoms right out of vessels that sail too close to it. The whole ocean floor is a grave-yard of ships."

"I don't want to hear that kind of talk," Sophie put in firmly. "Shame on you for saying these things to my daughter, especially on a beautiful summer day like today, with only gentle waves and a cool breeze blowing. . . . Look how beautiful the view is here, Jenny. There's City Island."

"Sorry, Sophie." Eliza bit her lip and frowned.

Jenny made faces at Eliza and clutched her mother's hand. "I like it here, but it's scary to be so high up."

"In a storm, the wind roars and the whole lighthouse howls," Eliza continued. "I've looked out my window and seen twenty-foot seas smashing against the side of the building and even reaching as high as the tower. Later we had to clean away the seaweed from the window-panes."

"Aren't you scared when the wind howls?"

"A little," Eliza replied. She pointed to a place out in the water. "Jenny, this is where, as a little girl like you, I tossed a bottle with a message in it."

"Did you ever receive a response?" Jenny asked.

"No," Eliza said. "I imagine the bottle shattered on the rocks. Things don't always work out the way you might want them to."

"Sometimes everything falls into place when you make an effort. All you need to do is take the first step," Sophie countered.

"If you don't fall on the rocks first," Eliza muttered.

"Eliza! I don't know what has gotten into you! In a

minute I may ask Sam to bring Jenny and me back to land. I don't feel you're here with us," Sophie continued. "Tell me, what is it?"

"You're right—I'm out of sorts." Eliza crossed her arms and sighed. Then she added, "Come, let's all go downstairs. Jenny can go exploring through all the rooms, and Sophie, I'll show you my newest drawings and paintings."

As soon as she and Sophie were alone in her room, Eliza went to her desk and pulled out two letters from underneath a stack of papers in the drawer. "I want to show you the correspondence I've received!" she whispered.

Eliza carefully took each letter out from its envelope, unfolded it, then handed it to Sophie. "This one's from Alfred," she said. "The other's from Charles."

"Alfred is marrying Carlotta, did you know that?"

"He told me! It's there in the letter."

Dear Eliza,

I have been the one assigned to take over your fourth-grade class until school ends for summer break. I hope you don't mind dreadfully much. The children miss you and ask for you often, especially Lizzie and Justin.

At one time I fancied you and I kept hoping you would change. I see now we are two very different people and it would never have worked between us. Carlotta and I are to be married in August. You will be receiving an invitation for our wedding. I hope you will be in attendance. I remain,

Your friend always,
Alfred Poofall

Eliza,

I miss you, my dear. Remembering the way you ran up the stairs in my mother's house makes me think of you in your lighthouse. I forgive you for whatever you have or have not done. I hope you will return to City Island, and to me, and accept this engagement ring, a token of my true love for you.

Charles Boxley

"Oh, Eliza! He actually proposed to you! Where's the ring?"

Eliza opened the desk drawer once more, and with a sigh took out a small velvet box, which she handed to her friend.

Sophie opened the box and fingered the small, delicate gold band inlaid with tiny blue gems. "Will you accept the ring?"

"Yes. Perhaps. I don't know, Sophie! What should I do? The letter came nearly a week ago, and I must come to a conclusion about the matter."

"You're very young, and it seems to me that you don't have a good basis for marriage. Nothing you've said so far indicates to me that you're truly in love with the man," Sophie declared plainly.

Eliza looked out at the water and said, "Charles would give me a good *life*."

"If you want to move back to the Island without marrying Charles, you could stay with my aunt and me and Jenny," Sophie said.

"I think it would hurt you. What would the schoolmasters think? Besides, I don't want to live with you unless I can earn my keep."

"How about going back to the parsonage?"

"Never! My mind is made up. I think I'm going to marry Charles."

Jenny returned to the room, breathless. She squinched her small, freckled face. "There's a dead turtle in one of the rooms!"

Eliza laughed. "Don't mind that old turtle. It's just part of Sam's horrid collection."

Sophie caught Eliza's arm and whispered, "Promise me you won't do anything rash. I want you to come visit me on the Island, and then we can talk privately."

"Well . . . there's nothing to talk about," Eliza replied. She unrolled some new drawings from a bundle of papers and spread them out on the floor. She was feeling more agitated by the minute. Any decision she might make seemed as though it would be the wrong one. She didn't exactly want to marry Charles. But she didn't fancy the idea of spending the rest of her life in the lighthouse. If she married Charles, she could at least live on the Island in dignity. Then, maybe, folks would forget about her having been expelled from school. Besides, Charles was a good man, and it would hurt his feelings if she refused him. What a dilemma! Eliza thought of Ralph, how he blithely waded his way through life. Wherever he was, he was probably having himself a grand old time. Why was life so difficult for her?

"Here, I want to show you my favorite piece of artwork," she said, leading Sophie by the hand to her easel in the corner of the room. "I've been painting it on a small pine tabletop that I found washed up in a storm. Careful, the oil's still wet."

Jenny pushed in front of her mother to see Eliza's painting. The board had been square, but its four edges had been cut off, making it into an octagon. The scene, on a circle at the center, showed the red brick lighthouse from the front—tower at center, bell and flag on top, surrounded by water, with trees in the distance. Eliza herself appeared as a small figure in a dory in the forefront on the right. She had created the scene a hundred times, yet this painting was somehow different, she thought—fuller, more interesting. It was as if, having now gone beyond the boundaries of the painting in real life, she was better able to capture what was familiar to her.

"*You* painted this?" Jenny said, awed.

"Yes, Jenny. Why are you surprised?"

Jenny wrinkled her impish nose.

"You made all this artwork in the month you've been here?" Sophie asked.

"One hour at this lighthouse is the equivalent of one day on land. Three weeks is like three months," Eliza replied with a sigh. "There's always cleaning and polishing to do. But sometimes in the afternoons I'm free to go fishing and collect mussels in the shoal water or make drawings and paintings. . . ."

"Eliza, we must continue to talk about where your life is going. You look so miserable. You're only seventeen years old. There's no reason to hurry a decision. Will you promise not to do anything rash?"

"I won't do anything rash."

"Look me in the eye. Tell me it is your unruffled decision to marry Charles Boxley."

"It is," she answered firmly. Then she added, as if to herself, "Can someone please tell me what other choices I have?"

When Sophie and Jenny had left for the mainland, Eliza took out her brushes and oils and put the finishing touches on the small painting. In the lower left-hand corner, she added some flowers for decoration.

"I've been making this same scene year after year," Eliza said out loud, talking to the painting. "That's me. I'm rowing away from this place, but I still haven't escaped it."

"Daughter, you are always welcome here. I wish you would not leave to be married just yet," Papa said.

"Wait a few years," Mama urged. "Girls are marryin' a little later these days. I was your age when I married your father. Then just about every year, I had a child. Are you prepared to have children?"

Eliza pushed the fish stew around on her plate without eating it. She didn't answer her mother's question.

"Most women lead wretched lives. Remember to count your blessings. Life could be much worse for you than it is already," Mama went on.

"I say she should go off to live in the woods with Ralph," Sam said.

"Leave me alone!" Eliza snapped.

"Eliza, never you mind your brother. Sam, go to your room," Mama ordered.

Sam gulped down his last drop of cider, rose from his seat, and stomped off.

Mama had been nicer to her since her return, Eliza reflected. It was as if Mama were saying: You left this place, you went out into the world, and you got hurt. Stay with me and hide. Side by side, we'll do our chores.

"One thing to keep in mind about your Mr. Boxley: It's a good thing to be with a man who has no financial worries."

"Are you suggesting I marry Charles? Is that it?" Eliza asked.

"You are a very ornery girl, Eliza. I said you're too *young* to be married. Wait until you're at least twenty. When you do marry, however, you may as well have the advantage of wealth, because many other things are sure to go wrong."

"She's saying don't marry someone like your father who earns a low keep," Papa interjected. "Isn't that what you meant, Mrs. Elsie Cavanaugh Brown?" A long strand of hair, usually combed across the bald part of his head, fell out of place, and there was fire in his eyes.

"That's not what I meant!" Mama replied.

"Life with you hasn't been a picnic either. Every day for twenty-six years I've been listening to your sassy tongue. I won't hear any more of it tonight," Papa said as he braced his elbows on the table and hoisted himself out of his chair. As Sam had done several minutes before, Papa left the room.

"Mama, why was it all right for Amanda Jane to marry the pastor but it's not all right for me to marry Charles?" Eliza asked.

"Your sister was a few years older than you," Mama answered.

"Tell me the real reason, Mama: You don't want me to be happy. You always favored Amanda Jane and you never cared about me," she said.

"That's not true. It's just that your sister has more in the way of good sense. There are so many things you don't understand. You will know better when you're a mother yourself someday."

"I'm going to marry Charles Boxley and I'm going to leave this lighthouse," Eliza said, but as soon as she uttered the words she felt in her heart that it was not the right thing. To be honest, she didn't know what she wanted.

Mama said, "You're as stubborn as your father, Eliza Charity Brown."

Chapter 22

June 1904

Another week passed before Eliza set foot on City Island. She proceeded directly to the Boxley residence, opened the painted wooden gate, and followed the cobblestone path around the side of the house to the Boxleys' favored side entrance. She caught a glimpse of Mrs. Boxley, arranging a vase of white roses. In the shade of the carriage house, Charles was almost completely hidden underneath his motorcar, evidently making some repairs. Eliza recognized his long thin legs and narrow feet. "Charles," she said softly, but he did not hear her.

Eliza waited and watched him for quite a while. She was glad to see him. "Charles," she said again, a bit louder this time.

Charles emerged from underneath the car, wearing a big grin on his sooty face. Since she had last seen him, nearly three months ago, he had grown a slim mustache. The mustache looks a bit silly, she thought. Poor Charles;

such things can't be helped. Then again, she mused, he's striking in his own way, really, with his lean, strong build.

"What a surprise!" Charles said happily. "I've often thought I would never see you again."

For an awkward moment, they just looked at each other. Then Charles took Eliza's hand and studied it closely. "You're wearing the ring."

"Yes," she said. It pleased her to see his grin.

"This is a happy day," he said. "Wait for me a moment. I'm going inside to wash up and I'll tell Mother you're here."

The warm June sun on her back, Eliza walked through the stone archway that led to the garden and seated herself on one of the painted wicker lawn chairs. The smell of flowers clung to the air. Everything was in bloom—apple trees, violets, daisies, hollyhocks, lilies, and white and red roses growing on a trellis. Mrs. Boxley did indeed have an artist's eye. In a semicircle, she had planted kitchen herbs—parsley, oregano, rosemary, mints, basil—and in a section toward the back were the vegetables, squash and tomato plants and even a delicacy, cucumbers.

Presently Mrs. Boxley came out of the house with a pitcher of iced tea and three tall glasses full of ice. In Eliza's glass she put a sprig of newly picked spearmint.

Charles had evidently told his mother of the engagement, for she seemed particularly cheerful and welcoming. "Is it too soon to speak? I'm glad you're going to be my daughter-in-law!" she said.

"So am I. I couldn't be more lucky!" Eliza said. She did feel lucky, too. Fortunately, neither Charles nor his mother seemed to care about the scandal with Ralph. Eliza guessed that Mrs. Boxley was happy that someone had finally agreed to marry her son. In a way, life couldn't have turned out more perfectly, Eliza reflected. She wondered why she hadn't seen the possibility before. She'd be able to hide forever in this lovely escape of a place.

Where was Charles? People said women took a long time dressing, but Charles beat the record of any woman, Eliza said to herself.

It was almost difficult to be still here. At the lighthouse there was never a moment to be lost, always a floor to be polished or swept. Here she would be tended to by a servant.

Charles did, finally, make his appearance, his mouse-brown curls now wet and clean and greased with hair tonic. He wore a striped shirt with a rounded starched collar.

"Shall I go and fetch the camera?"

No! Please don't take the entire day fiddling with your camera equipment, she thought. Still, she found herself saying yes. How devotedly Charles took photographs, how devotedly he kept his motorcar, and all his things, in good order, she told herself.

"Why don't you wait until later to take out your camera, dear?" Charles's mother said. "I'd like to have lunch brought out."

By and by, Edna served salad from the garden, along with sliced hard-boiled eggs and bits of streaky bacon. Then there were fish sandwiches, grapes, and slivered almonds. "Everything you do is magnificent," Eliza told Mrs. Boxley in true admiration.

Eliza dropped her napkin and nervously reached down to pick it up. As she did so, she noticed a short-haired gray cat from the neighborhood sauntering by. She caught its attention, then put a tiny bit of the fish on her fingers for it to lick.

As she chewed her food as daintily as she could, an image of Ralph, reclining in a hammock, came to mind. She quickly dismissed it. Thankfully, he had slipped out of her life and was probably somewhere very far away. Here at the Boxleys', everything was perfectly in place, and she loved it. Even the gravel of the carriage path was swept to perfection. It was far above any life she'd ever imagined for herself.

"Mother, I'd like to show Eliza the old servants' cottage. I'd like it to be our home when we're married," Charles said, and his mother nodded agreeably.

After lunch, Charles gave Eliza the tour of the cottage, which stood on the opposite side of the garden, adjacent to the carriage house. In it were five rooms on two levels. "There is no electricity in this house as there is in the big house, but I think I can arrange for it," Charles said cheerfully. "Maybe I can even have a telephone put in."

"A telephone!" Eliza said, surprised. She couldn't imagine living with one.

Together they walked around the bottom floor of the house. As the place was used for storage, there were boxes and crates crowding the floors. "This can be cleared out," Charles said, "and, easily enough, indoor plumbing can be added, as in the big house. In the meantime, there's the privy."

"There in the corner—is that a skull?" Eliza asked, horrified.

"We can put that somewhere else," Charles said with a laugh. "My father was a lawyer in Manhattan but he also fashioned gold teeth, and he filled orders here on the Island. He was an inventor of sorts."

"There's no oven in the kitchen," Eliza said doubtfully.

"No," Charles said, "but there's a fine kitchen in the big house. Mother won't mind it if you do your cooking in the big house. She loves cooking."

What if I want to prepare dinner for the two of us? she thought. Will the three of us spend all our time together? Once again, Eliza chastised herself, Charles had presented more splendors to her than she could have ever imagined. As wealthy as the pastor was, he did not have electricity in his house. Why, Amanda Jane would have been laid out in lavender before she would have ever guessed that Eliza would marry into such a family as the Boxleys.

"The bedroom's upstairs," Charles said, and Eliza followed him up the narrow, steep stairs. The room was empty except for faded lace curtains hanging loosely on brass rods and an oil lamp that was mounted to the wall. The wallpaper was mauve and pink, with golden pineapples.

Eliza walked to the window, with its view of the garden, and nervously fingered the curtains. She remembered the preparations for Amanda Jane's wedding, how she and her mother had helped to sew her sister new white cotton drawers and bodices and a cambric nightgown. A child every year, her mother had said. Suddenly Eliza felt herself growing flushed, and she thought she would be sick.

"Is everything all right?" Charles asked.

"It's just the heat."

I need not worry so, Eliza told herself. The man has, thus far, shown me gentleness and restraint. This methodical and meticulous man would be quite unlikely to exercise force. All in all, she reasoned, the decision to marry him was a good one, though how she was going to live on the Island again after the scandal, she couldn't imagine.

Eliza and Charles spent the rest of the afternoon at the parsonage, where Amanda Jane and the pastor offered their most sincere congratulations. Then Eliza visited Sophie. She found her with Jenny and several of the younger Horton cousins on the big lawn overlooking the water.

When she spotted Sophie, Eliza freed her hand from Charles's. Sophie said nothing at first, but Jenny, who was jumping rope with two slightly older girls, greeted her right away. "Eliza, I can jump on one foot now!"

"That's wonderful, Jen!" Eliza found herself answering in a falsely cheery voice. "Sophie, I've come to tell you Charles and I are going to be married."

Sophie offered Eliza her sparkling blue eyes and a look that showed some sadness. Without smiling, she said, "I'm glad you're back on the Island. Congratulations to you both."

Well, it will just take a little time for Sophie to adjust to the situation, Eliza thought. While Jenny was still jumping rope with her cousins, Eliza said her good-byes, and she and Charles returned to the Boxley residence.

"I must be getting back. My brother will be waiting for

me at the landing dock. I will visit again soon," Eliza told Charles when they were back in his mother's garden. She delayed, and leaned against the picket fence, waiting for Charles's reaction. Charles kissed her briefly, and his lips were red and wet, as she had remembered them.

"Time for one more kiss," Charles said.

Out of respect, Eliza agreed, then waited for the kiss to be over.

"When would you like to have the ceremony?" Charles asked.

"Perhaps next June?"

Though he was still in good humor, the look in Charles's gray eyes showed his dismay. He twitched his waxed mustache. "That's a whole year from now. I was thinking of this July, next month."

"Maybe December," Eliza countered. "I'll need time to prepare."

"How does September sound to you?"

"I'll consider September," she answered.

Then, before Eliza returned to the lighthouse, Mrs. Boxley took her hand and led her to the pantry behind the kitchen in the main house. She unlocked a mahogany chest and drew from it an enormous spoon, the kind used for eating in the 1700s. "This is the last of the flatware belonging to my great-grandmother, and I shall give it to you on your wedding day. Welcome to the family, my dear!"

Chapter 23

July 1904

"Papa, someone's coming. Look!" Eliza put down her rag, which was full of pungent brass polish, and wiped her hands on her skirts. Whenever she saw a boat approaching from shore, she felt a wave of panic run through her. There was always the possibility of bad news.

"A motorized dory with one passenger. I don't recognize the vessel," Papa said, looking through his heavy brass spyglass.

Eliza took the spyglass and followed the boat with one eye. An unusually heavyset man in a cap and blue uniform came into view.

When the boat neared the mussel-covered reefs outside the lighthouse, Eliza's father guided the visitor around the shallow, dangerous waterway to the safety of the landing dock. From the way the man adeptly maneuvered around the rocks, Eliza could tell he was an expert seaman.

Once the boat was safely moored, the man called out,

"Captain Brown, is it? I'm Captain Elijah Gildersleeve of the *Lizzie D. Bell*."

"You're welcome here, sir."

The skiff rocked precariously to one side when the captain stood and shifted his great weight to disembark. He seemed about seventy years old. With difficulty, he climbed up the metal ladder of the landing dock onto the base of the rocks. The side pockets of his brass-buttoned jacket bulged.

Eliza helped the visitor inside, Papa following close behind, and the two men shook hands. The captain caught his breath before attempting to speak.

"My ship is docked at the Robert Jacob Yard overnight for a few repairs. For some time I have wanted to come out here and meet you and your family, sir, and only now have I had the leisure."

The captain was the largest and roundest man Eliza had ever seen. As he talked, his small thin mouth and pointed nose moved within the large round mass of his face. He had brilliant aquamarine eyes and no upper teeth, though he appeared to have a full row of smallish bottom teeth. When he removed his cap, Eliza saw that his hair was bristly, white, and cut very short. It stuck up straight from the top of his head. The jolly captain resembled a blue-eyed bear.

"A rare pleasure to receive your company, Captain Gildersleeve. My wife and my son, the assistant keeper, are on land today. This is my daughter Eliza."

"Ah, Eliza! Eliza Brown! You've grown to be a beautiful young woman."

"Welcome to our home," she said, wondering why the

captain seemed to know her. "We'll go upstairs and I'll put on the kettle for some tea."

Eliza and Papa gave the captain a tour of the three small rooms on the first level of the lighthouse, then brought him up to the living room on the second floor, where they seated him in the most comfortable chair of the house. Eliza excused herself to go to the kitchen, then returned a while later with jam and scones and a steaming pot of tea. She poured the tea into three mugs.

"Many is the time I've sailed by your beacon. My crew and I always took turns with the spyglass, looking for the spots of color on your little rocky precipice. A wonder to have seen flowers in the middle of the sea!"

Eliza blushed. "They were my flowers." She told the captain how her brother Peter had once bought her a penny packet of seeds at the general store on City Island and how for years after that she'd put handfuls of dirt into the pockets of her coat whenever she visited the mainland. Each spring, she continued, she'd wedge the dirt into the cavities of rocks, and occasionally some flowers would grow, cornflowers or black-eyed Susans, though they would last only until the next storm.

"Your garden was a sight for sore eyes!" the captain exclaimed. "You did a good deed in planting it."

"I never knew anyone noticed!"

"To think I've been passing by here all these years," Captain Gildersleeve said, expressing Eliza's own wonder, "and now I'm actually *inside* your comfy home. Ah, I love to see a house so clean and shipshape. You're 'keeping the good light,' Captain Brown and Eliza Brown. Bless you."

"That we try to do," Papa answered proudly. "As you

can see, my wife makes sure the premises are in perfect order. The lantern itself is cleaned and polished daily, thanks to my daughter here."

"I knew a keeper in Maine who kept the good light up to the very moment his beacon was overwhelmed by the sea. What bravery I've seen in the Lighthouse Service! Have you rescued many souls, sir?"

"Mostly it's the poor intoxicated fool run aground in a small craft on the mussel beds. About every two or three years a larger vessel is stranded. The biggest rescue in our parts was seven or eight years ago when the *Charter Oak,* a three-masted schooner, ran aground in the shoal water off City Island and sank her cargo of gypsum rock. All, fortunately, were saved. Then many years ago we saved two in an overturned canoe. Eliza was the first to spot them. Just a little girl she was, skipping rope in the early morning. Isn't that so, daughter?"

Eliza nodded. "It's good to hear your stories, Papa," she said. Living the life he did, she figured, he must miss the company of men.

"In my lifetime, two ships I've captained ran aground on rocks in storms and were lost," said the visitor.

"I'm surprised you had the courage to go back to sea," Eliza remarked.

"You can't be too timid about your actions!" the captain replied with a toothless grin. "Life's an experiment. Sometimes you fail, but the more experiments you try, the better. That's what I say!"

"I suppose the flowers were my experiment. My paintings, too," Eliza added as if to herself. She didn't mention her adventures on City Island.

Eliza poured the captain a second mug of tea while she listened with fascination to the tales of his life. She laughed as she watched him devour two scones and lick the apricot jam from his fingers. He was a friendly, jovial man, all 304 pounds of him—his exact weight, he readily volunteered. Captain Gildersleeve had been out to sea since his boyhood, he said. His residence was Port Clyde, Maine, where he lived with his sister, two of his grown children, and several grandchildren. He was the captain of one of the cargo schooners that Eliza had often seen pass by the lighthouse on their way to or from Maine and New York, bringing wood and granite for tombstones south and returning north with coal. To accommodate the granite, the "tombstone schooners," as they were called, were specially built with their double masts spaced wide apart.

The captain stopped talking and gulped down the rest of his tea. He then opened a leather wallet and took out a few dog-eared photographs and said, "I've some pictures of the family that I always carry with me."

Eliza puckered her lips and tried to conceal her interest as she held the photograph of a young man. "Who is this?" she blurted out.

"That's one of my grandsons, Christopher Gildersleeve, a melancholy youth. I think he's about your age. I sent him off on a whaling ship. Ah, but he writes he is unhappy and will soon return. The great adventure of slaughtering whales is not for everyone, I suppose."

"And this photograph?" Captain Brown asked, pointing to a lady dressed in a lace shawl and a large feathered hat.

"This was my wife. She always wanted to live in a

lighthouse. I named my ship after her—the *Lizzie D. Bell*. It has indeed been the sorrow of my life that she took ill and departed this earth—to her well-deserved rest in heaven."

"The younger of my two sons drowned, just this fall," Papa said with remorse.

"Peter," Eliza put in. "His birthday is approaching. Had he lived, he would have been twenty-one years old this September."

"Aye, a cruel life it is sometimes. Many men I've known have grown cold-blooded living lives of tragedies from the sea," Captain Gildersleeve said with a sigh.

"But you never did, sir," Eliza said, marveling. How strange it was to be speaking so frankly to a man she had never met before in her life!

"When one of us takes a step forward, we all do," the captain offered. Then there was a long pause in the conversation, as if no one knew quite what to say. "Don't give up the ship!" Captain Gildersleeve added. "You see, I have come to visit you today because I found your bottle."

"Goodness! Where? When? I couldn't be more amazed than I am at this moment," Eliza said. "How is it that you found my bottle?"

"Seven or eight months ago I was out on the end of Long Island. The *Lizzie D. Bell* had made a delivery and was docked there. I happened to be on shore leave, and I was walking along the beach after a storm and found the bottle tucked into an inlet, mixed amongst some seaweed and driftwood. Many wonders I have found over the years, my dear."

Captain Gildersleeve pulled the bottle out from his pocket. He handed it to Eliza, and she slowly unwrapped the letter she had put there six and a half years earlier. She read her words as if she had never heard them before. *Write if you are able. I hope I make a new friend because on this island I am not able to have friends.*

"Here you have a friend. It's me!" said Captain Gildersleeve.

Eliza looked at the fat, toothless sea captain in wonderment. In the time since she had dropped the bottle into the Sound, she had made many friends, but there was room in her heart for one more. The world was certainly a marvelous place, despite everything, she realized. "Your friendship is most welcome, sir," she said.

"To me as well, Captain," Papa offered heartily. "You are always welcome here."

Next Captain Gildersleeve took from another pocket a package of brown paper and presented it to Eliza with a ceremonial bow. "Here, I have a book for you," he said, and beamed. "Remember? Your letter said, *Any new books and stories you might like to send me are greatly appreciated. I say this in case my letter finds itself in a wealthy hand.* Well, your letter found itself in a wealthy hand!"

"I'd given up hope of receiving an answer! Especially so many years later!" Eliza exclaimed. Then she carefully unwrapped the package. The book was a slim illustrated volume called *Sentinels of Our Coast*. "Thank you, Captain. You didn't need to bring me a gift!"

"A pleasure," the captain said. "Perhaps you'd have preferred a novel, but I wanted to show you something of my own coast and of the lighthouses there."

205

"I shall treasure it always." Eliza carefully turned the pages of the book. "I love a book with pictures. I didn't know there were so many different styles of beacons."

Captain Gildersleeve rolled his eyes around and stared at Eliza as though he had something important to say to her. "My sister is an itinerant teacher of lighthouse children. Some of the lighthouses are so far from land that the children cannot go to a regular school, so my sister goes to them, weather permitting. She spends a few weeks with each family."

"That sounds marvelous," Eliza said. "It would be ideal to teach only a few children at a time. When I taught at the City Island School, I had twenty-one children. Five girls and sixteen boys."

"Hosiah Prim tells me you also did quite an outstanding job," the captain added.

"You know *Hosiah Prim?*" Eliza said, mortified. Would her misdemeanors follow her even beyond City Island?

"Yes. I visit the Prims whenever I stop over on City Island. Hosiah's father was a friend and a fellow sea captain. This last stopover, I told Hosiah that I'd found your drift bottle, and he spoke quite highly of you," the captain said, and then paused. "You see, in addition to answering your letter, I have another purpose in visiting you today. My sister is an older woman, only about ten years my junior, and she could use some assistance. This is an odd request, but do you have any interest in such a position?"

The first thought in Eliza's mind was no. How could she break off her engagement to Charles and move so far away? Then a glimmer of hope entered her heart.

"Would your sister truly be interested in my help?"

"Certainly," he said. "You are welcome to come to us at any time, either for a short visit or for an extended stay if you wish it."

"I—never in the world imagined such a possibility could exist for me," she stammered. "I shall think about it. In any case, I appreciate your kindness. I hope you will leave an address where you can be reached, Captain. Why don't you write it here in this book?"

"I shall," he said.

"I have a gift for you, too, sir." Eliza rose from her chair and ran up the spiral stairs to her room on the third floor. There she found the oil painting of the lighthouse that she had just completed. She paused to look at it one more time, and to say good-bye to it, before bringing it downstairs to the captain.

"My daughter has become an excellent painter," Papa said proudly.

"It's a magnificent painting!" the captain agreed. "I shall hang it in my cabin on the ship, where I can see it always."

An hour later, the captain said his farewells and Eliza watched the dory disappear into the distance, thinking again what an extraordinary day she'd had. Perhaps there were many more bridges in the world than she had thought. It only seemed as if she were on an island, when in fact she was connected to people by mysterious forces—across water, and maybe even across time. She need only ask and wait, she realized, and truly she would find help and companionship.

When she could no longer see Captain Gildersleeve's boat, Eliza went inside and brought the book to her room. She looked at the illustrations of the different lighthouses, and thought about the families that must live in them. Maybe, she thought, she'd even meet those people someday.

Angels at work, she said to herself. An angel in the guise of a heavyset, toothless sea captain, a strange gift from God. A friend.

Chapter 24

*Letters from Eliza C. Brown
at Stepping Stones Lighthouse*

To Miss Julia Gildersleeve, Gull Road, Port Clyde,
Maine

Dear Miss Gildersleeve,

*Many thanks for your letter. I am overjoyed to know
I shall soon be the assistant to the itinerant teacher of
lighthouse children! The position seems more suited for
me than any I could imagine. I shall do my best to work
hard and be deserving of it. I have but a little experience in teaching, yet I care very deeply about books and
learning. The spark that began in me at an early age
when I learned to read has kept burning ever since. For
those children like myself who have not had much con-
tact with the outside world, their books and pen and
paper will always be their friends and their link to
humankind.*

*In the isolated existence I have lived, I find I am
dreadfully behind the times in many matters. I know
little of the latest fashions and inventions. I am, how-*

ever, well versed in the Bible and the classics, having had many solitary hours in which to study. I can draw and paint with proficiency. I have a sturdy constitution and am not often ill. I am definitely not of a timid demeanor. I can crab and spear eels and catch all varieties of fish and gut them. I can row a dory almost as well as any man. Perhaps this odd mixture of talents has served as good background for something, after all. To each of us God has given a purpose.

I look forward to meeting with you.

Until then,

Yours sincerely,
Eliza C. Brown

To Mr. Charles Boxley, Esquire, Prospect Street, City Island

Dear Charles,

There is a pull within me to see more of the world and so I must leave City Island for a time. I don't know if you will understand, dear Charles. I know it is important that I at least try to give some explanation in this letter, however brief and inadequate it may be.

So much of my life has expanded; you have been part of that. I return your ring with my sincere thanks. Recently my fortune has changed and I have accepted a teaching position in Maine. I hope you will not look upon our parting with remorse. Indeed I am terribly sorry to disappoint you. It is painful for me to think I am hurting your feelings, especially since you have taught me so much and have been so good to me. I remember the day you first took me for the long ride in your fine automobile and I saw my lighthouse from a distance. It was the most exciting day of my life. I say this with all honesty.

Know that I appreciate your kindness and your generosity. You are a modern gentleman in every respect.

Regards to your mother, of whom I am most fond.

Sincerely,
Eliza

To Mrs. Sophie Long, Horton Avenue, City Island

My dear Sophie,

How can I even think about taking the journey on which I am about to embark? It is like climbing the tower and taking a leap into the waves. To everyone else I must act sure and steady lest they set their minds to convince me to stay. You are the only one to whom I can say the truth. Though I know not whether this venture will be a success, I am certain I must give it my best.

Oh, my dear, you are the first true friend I have ever had. I might have spent the remaining hours of this life sulking at my chores of climbing up the stairways and polishing the lamp, unaware there might be another venue for me. You gave me my first opportunity to be a teacher. By your very presence, you have softened me with your patient and gentle ways. I think we must have come to this life as souls together, falling

*through one of the same holes at the turn of God's great
sifter.*

*Several blessings have come out of the one tragedy of
our Peter—your friendship most of all. Doubtless it is
the workings of the strange and anonymous Spirit, who
sends down fierce storms and yet gives us a plank to
which we can grab hold.*

*A year has nearly passed since Peter was taken from
us. I hope you will consider exchanging your black dress
for one of a color that will show off your pretty hair and
complexion. Peter would have wished it, of this I am
certain. I know of no suitor worthy of you, yet perhaps,
God willing, one good man may come along who will
not be far off the mark.*

*I think of you and Jenny often and with much love. I
send you kisses and the promise that I shall visit you on
the Island before my departure next month.*

*Your friend always,
Eliza*

To the Reverend and Mrs. Lawrence Sanderson, The
Parsonage, Trinity Methodist Church, Bay Avenue,
City Island

Dear Amanda Jane and Pastor Lawrence,

*My growing pains have been enormous this year. You
my dear sister and brother-in-law have both taken the
brunt of these growing pains. I have been trouble to you*

and indeed trouble to myself. Please know that I appreciate the service you have rendered by taking me into your lovely home. I hereby apologize in all sincerity for any problems I caused you.

I will make time to paint a scenic panel on the pastor's carriage before I leave for Maine. In any case, I must pay a visit soon to see if the sunflowers I planted are in bloom.

Captain Gildersleeve has promised me fare to return for a visit at Christmastime. How else could I ever have agreed to be away from your handsome baby boy?

Yours very truly,
Eliza

To Mr. Hosiah Prim, Principal, City Island School, Fordham Avenue, City Island

Dear Mr. Prim,

Many thanks for your kind reference to Captain Gildersleeve.

I'm enclosing my final essays for your evaluation. If you should find them worthy, please forward my diploma to my new address, as marked on the bottom of this stationery. That is where, as you know, I shall soon be serving as a teacher.

Cordially,
Eliza C. Brown

To Captain Elijah Gildersleeve, Gull Road, Port Clyde, Maine

Dear Captain,

I will never be able to thank you enough for showing me that in this life new beginnings are possible for those who have courage.

Your itinerant lighthouse teacher's program was surely an excellent inspiration on your sister's behalf. Would that we had something like this in our own parts for the children in offshore lighthouses here on the Devil's Belt. Someday I may well establish such a program myself!

I have studied the book you were kind enough to give me and look forward to seeing in person your beautiful and rugged coastline.

In the meantime I send you and your family my best wishes. Know that I am "keeping the good light" in the state of New York as I trust you are, even at this moment, "keeping the good light" in the state of Maine.

Sir, you are a true friend.

> *Yours ever faithfully,*
> *Eliza C. Brown*

Eliza rowed to the Island one Saturday in August to find that the sunflowers in Amanda Jane's garden were indeed in bloom. Most of the crimson hollyhocks had wilted, leaving room for Eliza's sunflowers to be displayed prominently against the picket fence. Three of them had survived the latest storm, though only the big one in the middle was still standing upright. Eliza propped up its head with a stick. The one on the left was broken and she couldn't do much to repair it; the one on the right was broken also, but two little sunflowers were growing out of it. A few dahlias, pink mostly, and one orange, still stood up proudly, along with a few black-eyed Susans. She picked two ripened tomatoes, then weeded a little, wondering why she cared about a garden she was not likely to see anytime soon.

Leaving the baby asleep in his crib and Amanda Jane and the pastor chatting with some neighbors, Eliza slipped away for a walk. She had written one more letter, to Peter, and wanted to deliver it herself.

Today marked the height of the raspberry season, Eliza saw as she walked down Main Street and crossed over to the fields bordering the Robert Jacob Yacht Yard. The raspberries fell to the touch, leaving yellow five-pointed stars on their spiny branches. She ate some of the berries as she walked. She wore her hair loose, and it was already becoming tangled. Mama and Amanda Jane must be right about always wearing a hat, she realized. And would she ever be able to go anywhere without getting a new hole in her skirt? Finally she reached the edge of the field, which looked down on the water and the shipyard. This was the place where almost a year ago she had watched Peter test the rigging on the *Reliance*.

Watching the men below outfitting the new yachts, Eliza tried to remember what the *Reliance* had looked like. It had been a beautiful, sleek yacht. Peter had been joyous that day, scurrying about with half the town looking on. His promotion at the yard probably meant he had come a step or two closer to becoming the captain of his own ship. She now understood that Peter had been following his dream.

Eliza hesitated for a moment before climbing down to the beach. Then, bending to pick up a shell, she turned to the sound of a friendly voice saying, "How do you do?"

"Ralph! I didn't see you there."

Ralph let out a deep, hoarse laugh. He was his same gregarious self, stringy long black hair, missing tooth, scars and all. He was clothed in a dirtied and worn sailor's uniform he must have found someplace. Or maybe he'd been employed on some crew during his lifetime? Eliza wondered. It was difficult to tell what was true with Ralph.

"You lied to me," Eliza challenged.

"About what?" Ralph asked nonchalantly.

"About *everything*, Ralph!"

"How could you say that about me? Don't you know how much I care about you?"

Oh, you devil, Eliza thought as she put her hands on her hips. She looked into the dark, narrow eyes peering out from underneath the long black bangs. He wasn't a bad man, really, she thought, and suddenly found she was no longer angry with him. Instead, she was sad that Ralph told stories about himself rather than putting his dreams into action. Yet the time she had spent with him had been magical. Something of the experience must have been authentic, she now realized.

Eliza told Ralph of her upcoming journey, and he seemed genuinely surprised, sad, and perhaps a bit jealous. "Maine? I suppose I'll soon be off to some faraway place myself. Good luck to you on your new venture," he said. Then he asked, "Where have you been hiding these days? In the lighthouse?"

Eliza nodded.

"I missed you," Ralph said, taking a step closer to her. He put a hand on her shoulder and fingered her curly auburn hair.

"I missed you, too," Eliza said. "This is good-bye, the last time we're going to see each other," she added, pushing him away.

He gave her a look of disappointment and surprise. She took a big gulp of air and dared to say the words in her mind. "I loved you, Ralph. I loved you so much I would have married you, if you'd had a job. You're a magnificent man. You're a truly special person, and there's no one in the world like you. Can you be magical without lying?"

"I don't understand what you mean," Ralph said gruffly.

"Think of that gold nugget you gave me once. I hope you do go mining for gold, because I'm sure you'd find some if you tried. I'll never forget you!"

Then, with a tug in her heart, Eliza continued to walk along the waterfront until she could no longer see Ralph. It was a blessing that she'd never received what she'd wanted from him, though it had all been very painful. Maybe, because he'd shown her what being in love felt like, she even had Ralph to thank for her not having married Charles, for whom she'd never truly felt any passion. Wouldn't *that* have been a life of isolation and entrapment, she thought, worse than the walls of any lighthouse?

From the pocket of her skirt, Eliza took out the blue glass bottle that Captain Gildersleeve had given back to her. The bottle was scratched, but it had fared well, considering its long sojourn. Eliza reread her letter to Peter before slipping it into the bottle and pressing down the cork.

To My Darling Peter, Lost at Sea,

The Sound is calm today and the sky the bluest and clearest I have seen in a while. How I wish you had lived to see this summer, with all its fine and breezy sailing weather.

Not a day goes by that I do not think of you. I often imagine that though I cannot with my mortal eyes see you, you are here somewhere nevertheless, floating about, carried bodiless by the crosswinds, now part of the elements.

I'd like to write a letter to you and toss it into the sea in a bottle, and seven years later receive a mysterious answer, as was the case with Captain Gildersleeve. Does one communicate with spirits in a similar roundabout way? Everywhere I look for a sign and everywhere I sense the presence of invisible hands, though I wonder if they're not of my own imagining. I never thought that I'd be the one to go to sea in a great ship. So be it, then. I shall set sail very soon, my dear brother. And if in my life I shall sail farther than you have yourself, it is only because you have gone before me.

Your loving sister,
As ever,
Eliza

Eliza took off her shoes and waded out into the water. Then, with full force, she threw the bottle as far as she could into the waves.

Chapter 25

September 1904

The evening Eliza boarded the *Lizzie D. Bell*, the first cool of autumn lingered in the air. The water was clearer than it had been in months. The gulls, which had not landed on the docks all summer, were moving inland. Snappers now flooded the local waters. Ever so subtly, the trees were beginning to change, a leaf here and there yellowing among the green foliage.

Eliza said good-bye to her father, then took the launch to the Island with Sam and Mama, where Amanda Jane, Pastor Lawrence, and the baby were waiting for them in the pastor's carriage. After they'd said their good-byes, Eliza stopped at Sophie's home before going on with her family to the shipyard.

The good-bye to her friend wasn't nearly as terrible as she had expected. It felt happy and sad at the same time; mostly the meeting felt hurried. Eliza cried a little, but they were happy tears rather than desperate ones.

Jenny, playing dress-up, wore an old pink satin dress of Sophie's, dragging its long train in the mud. Absorbed in her play, she did not say good-bye to Eliza at first. "Eliza is leaving for Maine tonight. It will be the last time you'll see her for a while," Sophie reminded Jenny. Upon hearing this, the little girl ran up to Eliza in her dirty dress and gave her a quick peck on the cheek. Jenny blew Eliza another kiss when she pulled away in the pastor's carriage.

Good-bye, Sophie and Jenny, Eliza said in her heart. A monarch butterfly flitted by, then another.

Eliza had sighted the two high masts of the *Lizzie D. Bell* from a distance. Painted blue, with a figurehead of a lady at the bow, it seemed a wonderful schooner to Eliza. Along the side of the ship was a stripe of gold.

The portly captain was there to greet Eliza at the top of the gangplank. He hailed one of the sailor boys to take Eliza's bag.

"Fine nor'west wind!" said Captain Gildersleeve, looking pleased that the evening winds had arrived.

The captain gave Eliza's family a tour of the boat and introduced them to the mate, second mate, and engineer. He showed them Eliza's cabin, which was small and clean. Then he pulled out charts to indicate the journey and explained the crew's various duties, their late-night and early-morning watches. The captain was obviously proud of his vessel, whose holds were loaded with a valuable cargo of coal.

"You will be helpful to the captain's sister? You will do as you're instructed?" Mama asked.

"Of course, Mama."

Sam gave her a smile. He appeared remarkably good-natured, Eliza thought. Oddly enough, she reflected, he seemed to understand her better than some of her other family members.

"Write us," Amanda Jane instructed.

"Keep us in your prayers," the pastor said.

Eliza wished Peter could have been there to see her off. Well, she said to herself, maybe in spirit he was.

When the family left, the captain offered Eliza a few kind words. "We're having a fine meal tonight at the captain's table, in honor of you," he bellowed. "Celery, salted pecans, olives, clear green turtle soup, broiled woodcock on toast, littleneck clams, caviar sandwiches, broiled soft-shell crabs, cold asparagus, stuffed tomatoes, saddle of venison, currant jelly, sorbet kirsch, fancy cakes, and cigars!"

"It sounds delicious," Eliza told him. "Do all sea captains eat so well?" No wonder he is three hundred and four pounds! she said to herself.

"Only when there's an occasion to celebrate. Of course, I try to find an occasion as often as possible."

There was much to do to prepare the ship for departure. Eliza watched the sails rise against the sky, which was pink, merging into blue on the horizon. A large steamboat passed and created a high ripple on the water, setting the ship to rolling back and forth for a few minutes. How excited Eliza felt to be going on a journey!

The captain took his place at the ship's wheel. Minutes later the vessel set off with a billowing grace. As Eliza took a last look at the crowd on the dock, she saw her sister holding the enormous baby Peter. He's going to grow up into a huge boy, Eliza thought. Would he remember her the next time she saw him?

The ship made its way out into the middle of the Devil's Belt. Eliza marveled at the number of rocks lining the coast; many more, she knew, lay beneath the waves. She caught a glimpse of the woods beyond City Island Bridge and thought for a moment she might have seen smoke from a campfire. Was it Ralph's? she wondered. In the swampland of Hunter Island, a large flock of egrets sat in the trees.

Then daylight turned into a beautiful black starry sky. It was frightening to be on a journey, but it was thrilling, too. Eliza gazed out into the darkness, and in the distance, though she could no longer see the shore, the beacon of Stepping Stones Lighthouse shone a brilliant, glowing beam.

Author's Note

Stepping Stones Lighthouse is a real lighthouse at the western end of Long Island Sound, where the Sound meets the East River. Nearby City Island lies at the tip of the Bronx in the greater New York City area.

City Island was once a thriving shipbuilding center, the place where several America's Cup boats were built, and even now it retains its nautical character. If you go to the south end of City Island to the seafood restaurants, you can look out and see the tiny red-brick lighthouse. At night you can see the lighthouse's flashing green light (which was in the early twentieth century a steady red light). The rocky little lighthouse island, alone in the water, can also be seen when you cross the Throgs Neck Bridge between Long Island and the Bronx. The journey from City Island to Manhattan, which now takes about forty minutes by car, took four hours by stagecoach less than a hundred years ago. City Island was then considered quite remote.

Though this story is fictional, there were a number of families who lived in Stepping Stones Lighthouse with their children from the lighthouse's construction in 1877 until it was automated in 1966. These children made the trip to school by rowboat, and they fished and speared eels. Like the characters in this book, lighthouse families were subject to the strict regulations of a national lighthouse board. Numerous other details in the book, such as Horton's Store, Ford's Candy Store, the Hell's Gate pilots, Burnsey's horse-drawn trolley car, and the outfitting of the *Reliance* at the Robert Jacob Yacht Yard, are all taken from historical accounts. Trinity United Methodist

Church and the old City Island School on Fordham Street, currently a history museum, community center, and condominium complex, remain City Island landmarks. Main Street now goes by the name City Island Avenue.

The painting on the book's back cover is an actual portrait of the lighthouse executed during the period in which this story takes place. It hangs in Iowa in the home of one of the granddaughters of Susie Gildersleeve, who was born in Stepping Stones Lighthouse in 1897 and lived there until her family was transferred to a lighthouse in Connecticut in 1903. The artist's signature reads "Horton, 1902."

Oddly enough, knowledge of this painting came to me after I'd written a first draft of the book. Seeking their family roots, two sisters, one from Iowa and one from Connecticut, had visited City Island. People in the local diner gave them the address of a history enthusiast, who happened to be a neighbor and friend of mine. Knowing of my interest in the lighthouse, my friend, Captain Fred "Skip" Lane, passed on their letter to me, and a correspondence began. On that exciting day when I received a snapshot of the lighthouse painting, my first thought was: Eliza did that painting! The following summer the sisters returned to City Island, and one windy June day, jostled about and sprayed by the rough surf, we all made a trip out to Stepping Stones Lighthouse in a small outboard motorboat.

This and other experiences I had during the writing of this book have confirmed to me that when you send out a message to the universe, as Eliza did with her bottle, the universe gives you back an answer.